RECKLE

Reckless Trilogy

Book 1

Lera Shishova

Copyright © 2025 by Lera Shishova

All rights reserved.

No part of this publication may be reproduced, distributed, or transmitted in any form or by any means, including photocopying, recording, or other electronic or mechanical methods, without the prior written permission of the publisher.

This is a work of fiction. Names, characters, events, and incidents are either the products of the author's imagination or are used fictitiously.

Book Cover by Lera Shishova

TRIGGER WARNING

Before you proceed, you should know that this book is intended for an adult audience, so if you're not an adult, you really should wait until you grow up. I swear, the book will still be out there when you do.

This book includes explicit sexual content. While all the sexual interactions are 100% consensual, not all of them are cute and fluffy.

There are a lot of scenes with on page violence and detailed descriptions of war in this book.

Minor trigger warnings include but are not limited to: family issues, mental struggles, strong language, death, etc.

I tried to make the trigger warnings as clear and inclusive as possible, but you never know what might trigger someone. So, in case my book traumatizes you in a bad way, I'm genuinely sorry.

This book is inspired by real life events but does NOT claim to be historically correct. This is a work of fiction and is NOT to be used as a textbook on any subject mentioned.

Happy reading!

RECKLESS DUSK

For everyone who has ever felt helpless despite doing their best.

I see you

PLAYLIST

Numb - Linkin Park

Bulletproof - Diamante

Here's to Never Growing Up - Avril Lavigne

The Strong - Eva Under Fire

Iris – The Goo Goo Dolls

Burn With Me - Lilith Czar

Break In - Halestorm

24/02 - Bez Obmezhen

Still Worth Fighting For - My Darkest Days

Festival - The Hardkiss

You're The One - Rev Theory

Paint It Black - Andy Black

Masterpiece - Motionless In White

Lifetime - Three Days Grace

Wherever You Wanna Go - Patty Griffin

PROLOGUE

All my 20 years, I was just a usual girl. I lived in a quiet, remote village with my mom. But what I knew, I always aimed for more.

Today, the 23rd of August, I woke up in my own bed. As usual. As I had been doing since the day I was born. Today is special, though. Today is the day I start chasing my dreams.

CHAPTER 1

SORRY, MOM

I stand in front of the mirror and look at myself. Blond hair falls on my shoulders and covers them. Grey eyes, pale skin. I'm wearing a plain dress and simple shoes. My mom says a girl should be modest.

I wish I looked different, though. Everything, including me, looks so usual, like nothing special is gonna happen today. However, I know it's not true.

I've never been a typical girl. While all my friends wanted to get married, settle down, and have kids – oh, well, at least when they were told they had to, they didn't argue – I knew that such a life was not for me. I've always known that.

Since I was a kid, I was fascinated by the stories about vampires. Their strength, powers, abilities... I've always wanted to be one of them. My mom never approved of this, as she said, 'insane' idea. That is the last thing she wants for her daughter.

Truth be told, she never really cared about me, about what I wanted and what I didn't want. She always says that one day I'll make peace with what I should be. I'm not sure she even knows me.

I go downstairs and enter the kitchen. My mom is already here. Even though I never considered her to be a perfect or even good person, I have to admit, she is the greatest cook I know. Even before I got to the kitchen, the smell of baked potatoes reached my nose and now I'm almost ready to eat them straight out of the oven.

When her brown eyes meet mine, she says, "Good morning. Did you sleep well tonight?"

"Yes, Mom, thanks," I answer automatically. So fake and formal. Well, if she only knew what I am up to, she'd never ever greet me that kindly.

Long ago, our region was divided among 5 vampire clans. After the war that led to that division, all the clans were way weaker than before. I don't know about other ones, but the clan that owns the territory where our village is realized that a good way to have new soldiers is to train humans and then turn them. It's been like that for as long as anyone alive can remember. From time to time, they just come to the village and take those who want to join with them. It was never obligatory for some reason. I wonder why. They definitely would have more people that way. Such soldiers probably wouldn't be very efficient, though.

Since I was a little girl, it was my biggest dream to become a vampire soldier. I remember once I said it to my mom. She was so angry I thought she'd explode. Starting with *'it's not for girls'* thing, ending with *'you'll die there.'* Well, eventually we all die, so don't see any reason for not going. Even after Eva – the girl who lives not far from us – told me some stories of what happened there. She went to the army a few years ago and returned after a month or two.

The stories that she told us really shocked my mom. What Eva said was that no one ever treated them as equals, not as people even. They had to work twice as hard as a normal person can in order to literally survive and get at least the slightest sign of approval from the clan leader, Arthur Black.

Eva said he was a real monster. When someone just started talking without permission, he could easily beat the crap out of the poor thing. The girl advised me to forget about this idea and to never ever even *think* of it again. However, do I care? No. Because how can I give up on my greatest dream that easily?

Today is the day vampires arrive, and I can finally join the army. I will. Whatever it takes.

I'm having breakfast with my mom. Nothing special – except for the heavenly potatoes, of course. However, my mind is on the train. The train that will take me to my dream.

My mom starts talking, bringing me back to reality. She surprises me too much by asking, "Do you know today is the day when vampires are coming to our village?" I didn't expect her to start this topic. "I hope you've given up your insane idea to join them."

I nod, but it's a lie. I just don't want to argue with her today. I know what I will do, and I know she'll never understand.

After a quiet minute, she adds, "Do you know that your friend Ruby is going to go?"

Ruby? Really? I almost choke. She is the least army-interested person I know. She can't even run a mile without saying that she's dying. Not very soldier-like behavior, if you ask me.

Surprised, I say, "Is she crazy? Is she really going to go?"

"Her mother wants her to," my mom says. "She thinks it will give her a better future."

It's total madness. Like, what?! Why should parents decide their kids' fate? It's so illogical, and irrational, and selfish.

"Will we see her off?" I ask, and she nods. It is a perfect chance for me to get to the station without raising any suspicions.

10 p.m. The train has just arrived. Its shiny grey surface is the stark contrast to our not so fancy village. It doesn't belong here, just like me.

A tall young man wearing all black steps out and says, "Those who want to go with us, come here, tell me your name and get on the train."

I am standing on the side of the platform, thinking of how I should get on the train in question. Ruby is nowhere to be seen. My mom notices Ruby's parents though, and we go to talk to them.

After exchanging a few pleasantries no one really needs, my mom asks about Ruby. "She's on the train already. I'm sorry you weren't able to say your goodbyes," her mother says, looking at me. "But maybe she will visit," she adds, smiling.

I know she won't, no one does. That's just not how things work. Why would anyone even visit the people who forced them to do the last thing they wanted? I will definitely *not* visit my mom.

"Anyone else?" the man in black shouts and when no one moves, the train's engine rumbles to life, and families start going home. It is my last chance.

So I just start running without so much as thinking about what I'm doing. I run as fast as I can and almost knock down a few people on my way. I can't miss this chance.

Right before departure, I jump through the almost closed door. The man is a little stunned, as I'm telling him my name. "I'm Lorna," I say, smiling like an idiot. He writes it down with an expression that tells me he couldn't care less about me.

The train starts moving and I look out of the open window. My mom notices me and starts shouting, "Stop the train! My daughter is there! She shouldn't go!" But of course the train doesn't stop. I wave my hand and step away from the window. It was probably the last time I saw her.

CHAPTER 2

WHAT IF THAT'S TRUE?

On the train, I find Ruby. "Hey," I greet her.

"What are you doing here?" she asks, her dull green eyes wide in surprise.

"Well, I'm more interested to know what *you* are doing here. Seems to me you never wanted this," I say.

She sighs. "It was my mom's decision, you know."

I sit next to her and hug her. "Everything's gonna be alright. I'm sure it's not as scary as Eva told us. At least we're together in this, right?"

"Thank you. You're always here for me. I appreciate that. No one ever is. No one ever understands except for you." I might not always understand either, but it's the right thing to comfort a friend.

I see a bunk bed right next to where Ruby sits on hers. "Hey, is that taken?" I ask, pointing and she shakes her head no.

I let go of Ruby and sit on the bed. "Now, it is," I proclaim and Ruby's red pained lips stretch into a smile.

The lights go out in a while, but during the whole night, I just sit near the window gazing into the distance. Sometimes I see nothing but darkness, so dense I assumed I went blind a couple of times.

But there were also huge cities, their glowing lights like a beacon in the distance. I've never been to a city before. I wonder what life there is like.

My mind is occupied with questions. What will my decision do to me? Was it the right one? Was it worth it? I guess I'll find out soon enough.

In the morning, we arrive. We get off the train, walk for some time through the woods, and then is the moment I'm actually stunned.

In front of us is an enormous gothic-style building with many annexes and a large territory. We're brought here for army training, but this isn't a military base, it's a goddamn art masterpiece. Its black-grey walls are so high I have to tilt my head to see the top. All the stone carvings and figurines... It'll take weeks, if not months, to give attention to all the little details.

The building is surrounded by a high stone fence, and woods around form another wall. With an open mouth, I go inside with the others.

Inside, it isn't less beautiful. High – *very* high – ceilings, exquisite chandeliers. From the inside, the building looks even higher than from the outside. It must have at least fifty stories. Okay, maybe a little less, but it's still enormous.

We stand in the foyer, and there are hallways and staircases that lead to all the possible directions. This place even has an elevator. An old gothic castle with an elevator. Vampires sure know how to combine the modern with the old.

While I try to take it all in, the man in black says, "Now you'll be led to your rooms. At 6 p.m. today, your instructor will be waiting for you at the gym."

Through long hallways, we go to what will be our rooms. The corridors seem very old because of the stone walls, but the lights remind that this building probably has all the latest equipment possible.

"You'll live four people in each room," the man announces.

I wonder who will be my roommates.

He stops in front of a room and calls four names. Mine isn't there. So isn't Ruby's. I do hope we'll stay together.

Next room. Ruby's here, but I'm not.

When he finally calls my name, I enter the room with three other people.

The room is pretty simple and quite small, all in light colors. Four beds and just one cupboard. Even though we didn't take much stuff with us – I don't really have anything – there's still too little space for four.

My roommates are a redheaded girl and two boys who seem to know each other well. They're probably from the same place.

I come to the girl and say, "Hi, I'm Lorna."

"I'm Grace," she answers. Her voice is very soft and gentle, even a little childish. Freckles dot her pale face, making her sky-blue eyes stand out. Her ginger hair falls in curls down to her chest.

One of the guys – the one with shorter, darker hair and brown eyes – comes to us and says, "Hey, girls! How you're doing?" He seems very happy to be here, his smile shows all his teeth, and he seems very friendly.

"Well, nice?" I say, a little bit surprised. "What about you? By the way, I'm Lorna. What's your name?"

"I'm Roy, and that's Memphis." He points at the other guy. "He might be such a pessimist sometimes, but he's not that bad," he adds, still smiling.

"I'm a pessimist only because I'm too tired of always getting you out of trouble," mumbles Memphis, his grey-blue eyes almost roll into his head, making me smile. "I guess they should make it illegal to have a second kid without the approval of the first one." He hugs Roy and rubs his head, the latter being shorter playing to his disadvantage.

"So you two are brothers?" I ask to clarify.

"Yeah, but you know, sometimes I think I have three parents," says Roy and laughs. I can't help but laugh, too. They all seem very nice. I hope we'll get along.

We still have time until 6, so we decide that it's a perfect opportunity to get to know each other better. We sit on the floor in a circle and talk about everything that comes to mind: origins, hobbies, favorite food, whatever.

Suddenly, Grace says, almost crying, "I already miss my family. My mom, my dad, and my little sister, Luna." She sobs. "I love them so much. I want to see them again."

I hug her to calm her down, and she lets me. "Hey, I know you miss them, but we're here for you, okay?" I say.

"Thanks, Lorna. I appreciate it," she says, still sobbing.

"I miss my parents too," says Memphis.

"Yeah, yeah, me too," mumbles Roy.

When I don't say anything, Grace asks, "What about you, Lorna?"

"Me?" I ask, surprised. "Not really."

"Why?" asks Memphis.

"I didn't have good relationships with my family," I reply.

The awkward silence hangs between us. Maybe I should tell them the truth?

Luckily, it's time to go to the meeting with our instructor. "It's almost six," I say. "We should go."

"Meet you instructor at the gym," I mumble, rolling my eyes as we wander the hallways for what feels like hours already. "This place is a goddamn maze."

"Yeah," agrees Grace. "They really should've given us some instructions on how to find it."

"Hey, have we been down this hallway already?" asks Memphis, pointing left.

"Yes," says Roy.

"Uh… I'm not sure," I say with a slight laugh.

We decide to check the hallway after all, but it's just another wrong one.

After more hallways and lefts and rights and wrong ways, we finally find the double doors labeled *gym*.

It is a large, spacious room, divided into a couple of areas. Fighting area, armory, some kind of area for athletics. It has large windows overlooking the forest. We're just high enough that we can see the treetops and a little bit of blue sky.

Our group has about 20 newcomers. I remember my mom telling me that it wasn't for girls, but there are many girls in the group. We are standing there, waiting for our coach, and no one has any idea who they will be.

Then the young man enters the room. He is wearing a grey T-shirt, black jeans, and combat boots. The sun makes his light brown hair – almost shaven at the sides – shine. He's nothing special, but his face looks so kind and somehow familiar.

I sign with relief that he must be our instructor. It could've probably been so much worse. But then he says, "So, you're all here to start your training and join the army, huh? In a couple of minutes, you'll meet your trainer. He's a busy man, he's late." He rolls his eyes slightly. "Don't mess up," he adds and smiles – his blue eyes warm – and leaves.

I am a bit disappointed that he's not our coach. He seems to be a nice and fun person. But well... We wait a little longer. And then he comes.

He looks to be about 27 or so years old. However, vampires don't age like humans do, so he can be of any age. He is so tall that my head will probably reach no higher than his chin. His hair is black as the feathers of a crow and is combed to one side, the strands fall on his face, covering it a little, and the hair on the other side of his head is very short, almost shaven.

He wears all black: a long-sleeved shirt, jeans, boots, and a cape. His hands and neck are covered with tattoos. This is obviously not all he's got, just the visible part.

And one more detail... His eyes. They are so blue and deep, I feel like I could drown in them. But they are cold – too cold to even belong to a living.

He stands in front of us for a while, and the first words he says are, "So, maybe you can finally shut the fuck up?"

Not even *'hello,'* not even *'how you're doing?'* I don't know, any politeness, no? Okay, whatever.

When we *'finally shut the fuck up,'* he continues... or starts, "I'm Arthur Black, and I'll be your instructor."

I can't believe my ears. Arthur Black himself will train us? After his words register, everyone starts chatting again. I literally jump when he shouts, "Silence!"

Eva was probably right, he is for sure not the nicest person I've met. "Tomorrow you'll start your training. I hope you've already seen your rooms because you'll live there until you become soldiers or leave. Up to you. See you here tomorrow at 6 a.m." He turns sharply and walks out of the room, leaving stunned silence.

6 a.m.? Come on, why so early? I think we'll sleep through all our free time here. We all go straight to bed after the meeting.

CHAPTER 3

WHAT'S YOUR NAME?

I lie in bed with my eyes closed. Through sleep, I hear screams. I sit up and understand that it's Roy and Memphis arguing. Turns out Roy wore Memphis' T-shirt, and it is an oh-so-huge problem. Brothers... I don't have siblings, so I will probably never understand.

Grace is still sleeping. Damn, how? I wake her up, and we go to the gym. This time it's a little easier to find, though I'd lie if I said we didn't get lost a few times.

When we enter, almost everyone is already there, however, we aren't late. In a minute or so, Arthur comes and announces, "Today's the first day of your training." Then he looks at Ruby and grins, "Nice heels. Do you think it's okay to wear them to an army training session?"

Since she was a schoolgirl, I never saw her wearing anything but heels, seems like they are a part of her – so is the bright red lipstick to match her dyed red hair she always wears in a ponytail – so the choice was predictable to me. Though it still makes me laugh a little. You must be a fool to wear heels – even not high ones – to a training session.

"Why not?" she says, "I like them."

"Okay, then you can start your training by running one circle around the gym in them. Go," Arthur says, still grinning. She doesn't move.

"Go or leave." His voice is calm. He isn't shouting, doesn't sound angry. But this cold, deadly calm makes me shiver. Ruby thinks for a moment more, then runs.

Well, *'runs'* is an overstatement, of course. Not many people can actually *run* in heels. I'm pretty sure I'd break a leg if I tried.

So Ruby is doing quite a good job, to be honest, even if I know it won't last long.

Arthur doesn't seem to care that she's running in heels though, she's too slow for him. Every few minutes, he yells at her to run faster. When she's done, he says, "If you want to be here, you have to follow rules, and for every stupid thing you do, there will be punishment." I do believe these words. "Now take them off, you look pathetic," he adds.

She takes off her heels with a defeated expression as Arthur turns his attention to everyone else. "So, now we can start the training. First, run five kilometers. You have five minutes," he says.

What? Running five kilometers in five minutes? He must be crazy. It's impossible. I share a worried glance with Grace.

Arthur comes to us. "Do you need a special invitation, girls?"

"Sorry, we just-" Grace can't even finish her phrase as Arthur slaps her in the face. She nearly falls but keeps her balance.

"No excuses. Go," he barks. We look at each other once again quickly and run.

At first, I feel just fine. I love running, so it brings me joy, though I have no idea how much I've run already or how fast I should go to even attempt to finish in 5 minutes.

Soon I begin to feel out of breath, and my lungs burn. My legs are so heavy it seems that they're glued to the floor. But I keep running. I don't stop. I can't stop.

"Five minutes up," rings Arthur's voice. We all stop and I feel like I'm dying. Everyone feels this way, I guess. And we didn't even do the whole distance. *Obviously, we didn't, we had too little time*. Arthur probably thinks we're professional athletes with supernatural abilities.

Suddenly, I feel like I won't make it here and I will have to return to my home village. Tears well up in my eyes, and I blink them back. I can't fail. I won't go back. There's simply nowhere to go.

After running, we learn and practice some basic battling things. Arthur explains every little detail with a ridiculous precision. He even follows his instructions with a demonstration, and his movements are so smooth it seems he doesn't even need to put any effort into performing them – which is probably true because it's just the base. But when I try to repeat them, it looks like I'm just fighting air and I'm losing. I didn't realize it would be so hard.

When the training session is finally over, we stand in line, and Arthur says, "Well, that was bad enough to expel you all." I hold a breath.

"However, I'll give you a chance." How very kind of him. I roll my eyes.

Everyone starts chatting. "Silence!" Arthur shouts. "I'm actually very excited. What are you all talking about? Come on, I want to hear what you say! Share it with me!" he challenges. He sounds like what's happening amuses and annoys him at the same time.

No one dares to speak but me. "Don't you think these tasks are too much for those who have never even tried such things before?"

He laughs wickedly and heads toward me. "What's your name?"

"Lorna," I say confidently.

"So, Lorna, you think you can talk to me like that?"

"Why not?" I ask. "You're not a god."

He hits my face. Hard. My cheek burns. "I hope next time you'll be smarter," he says, his eyes drilling through me. After a few heated seconds, he walks back to stand in front of us. I feel my body instantly relax, and I sigh internally.

The first rule to remember here: *'Don't mess with Arthur.'* Well, I don't care. I say what I want and do as I see fit. It was always that way. It was just the first time I broke this 'rule.'

CHAPTER 4

I TASTE BLOOD

I'm sitting on my bed, exhausted after yesterday's training. I rub my face with both hands and look down to see my knuckles bruised and scratched after punching a bag. We were learning how to fight again. Arthur told me if I go on like this, I'll die during my first battle. How supportive of him. Even though I already feel like I'm dying, I'll work harder today.

It's time for our first fight, even though we only had three training sessions – including today's one. We stand in line, and Arthur scans us. "Well, well, who wants to be the first?" he asks and then adds without a pause, "No one? Okay. Lorna, come here." I think he's hated me since the first day. Since I was brave enough to talk back. Or probably I was just stupid.

When I enter the fighting ring, he calls the name of my opponent. It's Grace.

Asshole. He must've realized we were becoming friends and started caring about each other.

We stand in front of each other, and we both understand that if we don't fight, we'll probably get killed. Seriously, it looks like that.

Even though we clearly don't want the other to hurt, we start. We rush at each other a little bit hesitantly. She tries to hit me, but I dodge. I hit her on the back of her leg, and she falls to her knees. I hope I didn't hurt her much.

She gets up, but Arthur stops us by raising a hand. "Well," he says, "that was an example of how you shouldn't fight. Unless you want to get killed, of course. Next." I am really surprised he let us go that fast. Am I missing something?

We watch everyone as they fight, and when everyone did, we start all over and then again and again. At the end of the training, I am completely covered in bruises and scratches after fighting 4 more opponents. Our lack of experience makes us do stupid things sometimes. I tried to hit one guy in the jaw and ended up hurting my hand of his teeth. Pathetic, huh?

Roy tripped over his own leg and fell, earning a hit on the head from his opponent. I don't even want to mention Ruby hitting her head on the pole while dodging a blow. At least she took her heels off... And now she's barefoot – because she doesn't have any other footwear – which is just as ridiculous.

Anyway, I probably need more damage, so I decide to speak up again. "Arthur, don't you think it's too much? We're humans," I say, looking at my bruised and bloody groupmates. "We don't heal like vampires do."

"Really, huh? Never heard about that." He seems to be amused by what I say. "If you're so brave, why don't you fight me?"

Without saying a word, I go to the ring. I try to act confident, but inside I'm shaking. If I survive, it already will be a victory.

Before I've even taken in what's really happening, he tries to hit me on my right shoulder, and somehow I manage to dodge. But the same second, he hits me on my left one. I manage to keep my balance, but he hits me again. This time my jaw. I taste blood. Before I can react, he sends me to my knees. He's too fast for me.

I get up.

The very second I do, I get a punch to the head. I stumble to the side to regain my clarity. This blow was harsh. Just as I turn to

Arthur, he sends his hand into my stomach. I manage to block the blow. Without hesitation, though, he delivers one more blow to my throat. Air leaves my lungs, I feel like there's no more left in me that I can use. I fall to my knees as I cough.

I take a gulp of air and get up once more. I might be bad at fighting, but I'm good at not giving up.

Another blow and one more and more and more... He sends me to the ground, but I get up over and over again. This happens until I can't stand on my feet. I feel dizzy and my vision is blurred, but I try to get up, anyway. I'm stubborn as hell.

But soon my body lets me down and I literally can't stand up no matter how hard I try. I hear Arthur's voice: "That was awful." Well, it really was.

But when I look up at him, I see something in his eyes that has never been there before. Respect?

Roy comes to me and helps me to my feet, and we get back in line. I lean on him for a while, but then let go to stand on my own.

"Anyone else?" Arthur asks. Everyone is silent.

CHAPTER 5

A STRAY

Me, Grace, Roy, and Memphis have already become friends. Now that we have some free time, we decided to go for a walk to find out what's interesting around the castle. However, the thing is that we're not allowed to leave its territory. So we had to sneak out while no one was looking.

When we're outside the fence, I say, "So, where will we go first?"

"I've seen a lake not far from here while we were on the train," suggests Grace.

"Okay, then. Let's go there," I reply.

We're walking through the woods. The rays of light break through the branches. I can smell pine needles. I can imagine how eerie this forest will look at night when the light from the sun is replaced by that of the moon. Trees will start resembling monsters with crooked limbs, and every rustle will make you shiver. But now it's peaceful, light, and vivid. It's really good here.

Soon we approach the lake. It is surrounded by woods. The water is crystal clear and mirrors the surroundings. There are high mountains on the horizon. Every time I see them, I think of how much I want to go mountaineering. I know my body isn't nearly prepared for something like that, but my spirit aches for it. Who knows? Maybe I will do that someday after all.

We sit on the shore and just watch the beautiful landscape in silence.

After about half an hour, Grace stands up and goes to the end of a wooden deck. She looks around, probably admiring the view.

Roy doesn't waste time as he jumps to his feet, runs to her and pushes her into the lake.

She falls with a huge splash. "Are you crazy?!" she screams as she surfaces. Roy just laughs.

Quietly, I get to where Roy stands and I can't help but push him into the water, too. The son of a bitch deserves it.

He falls next to Grace and laughs. "You reap what you saw," she says, pointing a finger at Roy. He rolls his eyes but keeps laughing, anyway.

Memphis comes to join me on the deck. "Don't you dare," I warn.

"I mean," he singsongs, "you did shove my little brother." He smiles apologetically and tries to shove me. I'm prepared though. We start fighting jokingly and our training kind of shows. It's not that we're actually hurting each other, but our moves are rather precise and not awkward and weird as they would be if we weren't training.

He manages to trip me after all, and I fall into the water.

"Welcome!" Roy says mockingly as he wraps an arm around my shoulders.

"Memphis, why don't you join us?" I drawl.

He smiles and jumps down to us. The second he lands, I splash him right in the face. He wipes the water off it and asks, "Satisfied?" I nod enthusiastically with a smile that shows all my teeth.

We splash each other and swim for some time before we decide it's time to finally head back.

While we were walking, the dusk came. Trees are illuminated with an orange glow from the setting sun. The forest looks even more magical than it did during the day.

By the time we reach the castle, it's already dark. I hope darkness will help us to not get spotted.

All our clothes are wet, and even a little gust of wind makes me shiver. It's just the early spring after all. It doesn't get too cold in this region, but it still can get rather chilly.

We enter the building the same way we snuck out – through the underground garage. The place that looks like a fucking heaven with all the sleek cars, bikes and military vehicles. We get to the foyer, and I sigh with relief that no one noticed us. We made it.

And then I hear his voice coming from the shadows, "Where have you been?"

I freeze. I see Arthur leaning against the wall.

"I asked a question," he demands as he stalks toward us.

"We were just walking," I say.

He slaps me in the face. "Walking? Who told you you could do that?"

We're all silent. His voice is strict and demanding when he asks, "Whose idea was that?"

No reply. I see his eyes go from me to Roy, then to Memphis, and then to Grace. "If you think you're going to act like fish and I'll just let it be, you're wrong."

"It was my idea," I say confidently. Grace looks at me with fear evident in her eyes.

"Not just hers," says Roy, "mine too."

"And mine," adds Memphis.

"We decided that together," finishes Grace.

I suddenly feel a surge of affection towards them. I love that we stand up for each other, but I still don't want them to get hurt. I could've taken all the blame myself. At least, my relationship with Arthur is already bad enough to not be afraid to make it worse.

"Alright," he says coldly and slaps Grace. She staggers back a step.

He hits Memphis in the jaw and punches Roy in the stomach, he doubles over from the blow.

Then he comes to me and grabs me by the throat and almost lifts me in the air. I grab his arm, trying to free myself, but he's too strong. I feel his cold fingers on my neck and his icy eyes piercing through me. A weak moan escapes my lips. I can barely breathe.

"If any of you pull anything like that again, I won't be so gentle." He looks at my friends and then back at me. He lets me go, and I fall to one knee and gasp for air. Then he leaves.

I lie in bed and can't fall asleep. I think of today's events. I should probably think of my family, of the place that I call home to make myself feel warmer. But I just stare blankly at the wall. What home would I think of if I never had one? What family if my father left me and for my mother I was just a duty she never wanted? I do need to feel warmer right now, but back 'home' I never felt that way.

For a brief moment, my mind drifts to Arthur and his cold fingers around my neck but I chase the thought away, I feel sad enough even without him on my mind.

I can't yet – if ever – call this place home but I feel much better here, even if I'm a stray anyway. This feeling just never leaves, it's engraved in my bones.

Well, if I have to be a stray, then I'd rather be a stray here. At least here I have friends.

CHAPTER 6

REBEL

Tenth day of training. We're throwing knives today. It turned out to be harder than I expected. Even if I hit the target once in like 10 tries, I hit it not hard enough and at the wrong angle, so the knife always falls. In the last hour, I've only done it once by pure accident. I'm doing much worse than others. I know I have to do something about it.

At the beginning, there were 23 of us, now there are only 19. Four have already left.

I don't wanna leave. I can't. I understand that if I want to stay, I have to try harder. Way harder. But I almost don't have free time... Except nights. So that's when I'll train. I'm starting today.

When everyone is in beds, I wait a little and then sneak to the gym. I'm not sure we're allowed to be here at night.

I look around at the dimly lit room. A shiver runs through me from my fear of darkness. But despite the fear, I also feel fascinated by it, so I decide not to turn the lights on.

I do some running first to warm up. I go for 10 circles around the gym. I wish I had a way of knowing how long it takes me. In big cities, people have so-called communicators with a lot of different functions, including time. I never had one, but a woman from my village did. She used to give it to all the kids so we could play. It was really fun. Anyway, even if I did have one, we were required to leave all our technology at home.

When I'm done running, my feet feel sore. I decide to let them rest and try the damned knife throwing. I grab 3 knives and stand facing the target. I look at it as if it can understand me and the threatening gaze I direct at it. "I can do this," I whisper to myself and let the first knife fly.

The knife meets the wall about a meter from the target and falls to the floor. I sigh. It will take time. *A lot* of time.

I try again. This time, the knife lands in the wooden wall. That's something. It's way lower than the target, but at least the knife didn't fall this time.

I throw the third knife. It lands in the wall as well. I guess I'm at least beginning to understand how to make it stick.

I go to collect my knives and repeat the procedure over and over until all knives end up embedded in the wall at least 5 times in a row. I hit the target only occasionally, but it's not my focus tonight.

After knife throwing, I get to practicing some fighting moves. I train until I'm sweating from head to toe and my body hurts.

When I'm back in my room, I'm completely exhausted. I glance at the clock and realize I've been training for 3 hours. I fall on my bed, not even bothering to take a shower and drift off at once.

Today, Grace woke me up because I simply couldn't wake up on my own. I was too tired after the night. I still am. I quickly take a shower to not stink like a pig, grab a quick breakfast, get dressed, and we go to the gym.

"Yesterday, you've learned how to throw knives and hit the target." At the words 'hit the target,' Arthur looks at me. I barely hold back from rolling my eyes. "Today, we'll see how much you trust each other. Lynn, stand in front of the target."

"What?" she asks, her green eyes rounded in obvious fear.

"I said, stand in front of the target," he says, his voice sharp.

She goes to the target. "Can I choose who will throw?" she asks.

"No," Arthur replies, "I will choose. Lorna." I almost choke on the air. Does he want her dead?

"I disagree," says Lynn. It's the first time she dared to talk to him like that.

"Don't your trust you fellow trainee?" Arthur asks, grinning.

"I... I... she's just not really good at that thing." Her voice trembles.

"Then you may leave," he answers calmly.

"Please, just let it be anyone else. Can Randy do that?" She's almost crying now.

Randy, the blonde, blue-eyed guy who lives with Ruby, is surprisingly good at everything. No wonder she chose him. I throw a quick glance at him, but his face doesn't show a single emotion.

"Do Randy and Lorna sound similar to you?" asks Arthur in his calm, cold voice.

"I don't want to get killed," she replies, more confident this time. Looks like the fear of getting stabbed in her is worse than her fear of Arthur.

"Then you've chosen the wrong place to do so," he says like a sentence. For some time everyone is silent, and then he adds, "Don't you know where the door is?"

"It's not fair," I finally speak up. "She shouldn't be blamed for the fact that I'm not good enough." What the hell am I doing? I glance at Lynn, and she nods and smiles weakly.

41

Then I look back at Arthur when he says, looking at Lynn, "You leave anyway. You don't follow my orders. That's the base. I am your leader. My word is law to you."

"Even if what you say is madness?!" I can't hold back my anger as I see Lynn leave. I know, I'm crazy.

"Who do you think you are? Why do you think you're allowed to do anything you want? A leader is not someone everyone's afraid of. But you probably don't have anything else to offer."

He seems to listen to me, and when I finish, he says, "Have you finished?"

"For now," I say sharply, meeting his gaze head on.

"So, you're brave enough to talk to me like that. That I already know. Will you be that brave to stand in front of the target?"

I take a breath and go to the target without saying a word.

I stand in front of it, wondering who will be throwing. It will probably be Jerry. He misses all the time. Does even worse than I do. But Arthur doesn't name anyone. Instead, he just picks up knives himself.

Is he going to kill me?

I try to keep calm and look confident. But it's pretty hard when the one who hates you holds a bunch of knives and you stand in front of the target. When you literally are the target yourself.

Then he throws and I flinch slightly. Knives hit the wall behind me one by one. Five knives not farther than a millimeter from my body. I blink and slowly let out a breath. I want to close my eyes, but I can't show that I'm scared.

He takes one more knife. A throw. And I feel sharp pain in my left hand. He hit my palm. I bite my lip to keep from crying.

He approaches me, never breaking eye contact. "When will you learn the lesson, Rebel?" He says and pulls the knife out of my hand. Unable to hold it inside, I groan. He hands me the knife, and I take it with my shaking, bleeding hand. My fingers aren't supposed to be able to hold anything, but they do. It's probably shock.

Till the end of the training, we just throw knives. And I battle with my palm. The blood hasn't stopped yet. Of course it didn't, I have a fucking hole in my hand. I wipe it off my T-shirt from time to time. If it wasn't black, it would probably be red by now. At least I got used to the pain and an uncontrollable twitch my fingers make from time to time.

"Hey, maybe you need to visit a doctor?" whispers Roy next to me.

"I-" I open my mouth, but Arthur cuts me off, "Do you want to follow your friend's example, Roy?" He looks meaningfully at the door, indicating what he means. We just continue throwing.

In some time, I feel like I might lose consciousness. It's probably blood loss. A hole in a hand is not really good for your health, after all.

When the training session is over, Roy reminds me about the doctor. I don't really want to go – I don't really like doctors – but he's probably right.

The hospital building is much smaller than the main one and looks more modern. I'm walking through a long white hallway, trying to find the right room. Room number 46. The doctor I met when I entered told me I had to go there.

I knock on the door before opening it. "Hello?" I say.

"What's your name?" A woman asks immediately, surprising me. She looks about 40 years old. Her greyish hair is short, and her eyes are dark, almost black.

"I'm Lorna. Why is it important?"

"Did you come here to ask questions?" she asks, clearly annoyed.

"Um, my hand's wounded," I say.

She looks at it. "Human," she spits.

"Yes, I am! Can you help me?!" I already want to leave.

"Sit," she orders.

I sit on a bench. It is so cold I shiver. She takes some bandage and something like iodine, but not exactly. When she applies it, I literally feel my hand begin to heal faster. Must be some vampire invention.

After she's finished, my hand stings more than it used to. "You shouldn't use your hand too much for a week at least," she says.

"What about the training?" I ask.

"I don't care. A week," she says.

"Thanks," I spit out and leave.

Awful place. I will never go there again unless I'm dying. No, not even then. I can't miss training sessions for a week. Not even a day.

"How's your hand?" Roy asks when I enter our room.

"I'm fine," I say. "Where are Grace and Memphis?" I ask, noticing they're not here.

"They went for a *walk*." As he says this, he smiles in a way that I understand that 'walk' probably means a date.

CHAPTER 7

THEY SHOULDN'T KNOW

When I woke up, my palm hurt even more. Probably after my night training. But I don't really care. I was waiting for Arthur to say some sarcastic shit about my hand during the whole training session, but to my surprise, he didn't.

After the training, Abigail and Ruby invited me, Grace, and Jess for a girls' night. I'll skip my training tonight.

When I enter their room, Jess — the short blonde girl — is already there. "Hi girls," I say.

Someone jumps at me from behind. I nearly hit her when I realize it's Grace. My hand stops midair.

"Am I so scary?" she asks, giggling.

"When you jump at me like that, you are." We all laugh at that.

We made tea, and now we're sitting on the floor, talking about everything. We've already discussed our families, our hobbies — apparently Grace loves drawing, the training. I finally told them about my nighttime adventures.

"So that's where you go each night. I thought you had some romance going on." Grace laughs.

"Come on, no," I protest. "No way."

"Okay, okay," she says, "But are you into Arthur?"

I nearly choke. "What? Why do you think I even like this idiot?" I answer with surprise in my voice.

"Well, you'd look good together," Ruby says, twisting the red lock of her hair between her fingers. "He's hot, isn't he?" she adds with a sly smile.

"Well, uh... he definitely is," I admit. "But if you're talking about a relationship, I'd like to date a good person, not a beautiful body."

"You know, I'd spend a night with him if I had a chance," Abigail says, her brown eyes bright. "What about you, girls?"

"I have a boyfriend, but even if I didn't, I wouldn't do this either. He's not my type," says Grace.

"Boyfriend?" asks Jess.

"I'm dating Memphis," she says shyly.

"I'm so happy for you," I say. Even though me and Roy suspected it, it's still quite a revelation. "He seems to be nice," I add. We smile at each other.

"Anyway, Lorna, what's about you and Arthur?" Abigail probs.

"Yeah, would you sleep with him?" Grace nudges me with an elbow.

"I wouldn't," I say sharply, maybe even too sharply. "Why are you keep trying to assign him to me? We really hate each other, can't you see that?"

I hope they don't see how shamelessly I lie. I can't explain why, but I actually do like him. He isn't the best person I've met, but somehow he is the only one who catches my eye. Maybe I can somehow see under his skin, and I feel attracted to his soul he never shows? Or maybe I'm just an idiot who is attracted to assholes. Yeah, that's more like it, and I really hate that. I can't believe I'm into some jerk when there are so many good guys. I deserve someone better. I do.

"I wouldn't sleep with him because I don't sleep with those who constantly piss me off," I conclude, and we all laugh. I don't want anyone to know about my feelings for him. It's better that way.

CHAPTER 8

UNAFRAID

Twentieth day of our training. We're learning how to shoot. I hit the target way better now. My night training sessions have already paid off. And my hand doesn't hurt so much anymore. The gun feels steady in my hand, and I am kind of enjoying it. Maybe I'm not a lost cause after all.

After the training, we have plans with Roy, Memphis, and Grace. At about 7 p.m., I'm waiting outside the main building when I see Roy.

"Hey." I hug him. "So, where are our lovebirds?"

"Probably doing their love things." He laughs. I roll my eyes. Then I hear Grace's laughter and turn my head.

"Sooo, are you ready to break some rules?" she almost sings the phrase.

"Hell yeah! Let's do it," I answer.

We have to take the train to get to the sea because it's unfortunately too far. We get to the station where we arrived when we first came here, and after about 20 minutes on the train, we're at the spot.

"Catch me," I shout and take off running. I look over my shoulder and see the guys follow me. Roy catches up to me first but stumbles and face plants the dirt. I laugh and keep running.

We come to the top of a cliff. I look down, breathless. It's as high as a five-story building, if not higher. I'm not afraid of heights, but I don't feel exactly relaxed knowing I'll have to fall down. The water below me is so clear I can see rocks at the bottom and I hope it's deep enough here.

"I'll go first!" Roy shouts. And I see him fall towards the water and disappear in it. In a couple of seconds, he is on the surface. Looks fun, to be honest.

"You know, I won't jump," says Memphis, shifting uncomfortably.

"Come on, are you afraid?" Grace gently pushes him out of her way. "Look how it's done."

Long fall, and she joins Roy in the water. "Lorna, come on, you're not afraid, are you?" she shouts. I barely hear her because of the wind that picks at my newly dyed dark blue hair and the sound of waves.

"Are you, Lorna?" repeats Memphis tauntingly.

Saying nothing, I step closer to look down one more time. Am I afraid? I am. But I can't show it. I can't let the fear stop me.

Now or never. I take two steps back and then run towards the edge. I jump.

For a second or two, I feel like I'm frozen in the air, and my body feels heavy, and then I fall down like a stone. *Splash*. And I'm in the water. I adjust my eyes and swim towards the surface. I'm alright.

Roy gives me a thumbs up, and I smile. We decide to go again.

When we've climbed up, we immediately start trying to talk Memphis into jumping, which makes him really uncomfortable judging by the way he speaks and acts. Seems like he's embarrassed that he's afraid. Honestly, I do understand why he is afraid, but I don't understand why people don't fight their fears and don't accept them either.

"Memphis, it's okay, it's really not that high," Grace pleads.

"Yeah, bro. You're missing all the fun," says Roy, disappointment lacing his words.

"Why do you even want me to jump? You like it? Go ahead. Why drag me with you?" says Memphis, already visibly annoyed.

"Come on, guys, really," I say. "Leave him alone." I also wanted us all to have fun, but talking him into it already feels like a waste of time.

I step away from them and get closer to the edge once again. I look at the distance, to where the darker blue of the sea meets the bright blue of the sky, and I realize that I'm actually happy. There are a lot of difficulties and a lot of things that I wish were different, but the thing is, I feel like I'm on the right way. I'm doing something that I really enjoy. With more training, I'm sure I will be able to achieve all that I aim for. I smile to myself.

But most importantly, I feel free. Despite all the restrictions and obligations, I feel free and capable of literally anything if I only try hard enough.

With this thought on my mind, I push from the edge and fall face-first into the ocean. My face stings a little as I hit the surface – I've never been good at face-first king of jumps – but I don't care much. I'm used to pain already. And not gonna lie, in some sick way I like how pain feels. Makes you feel alive, I guess.

When we get to the castle after some more jumping, before we even manage to get to our room, some girl tells us Arthur wants us in his room to talk. Somehow, he always knows when we break the rules. There were only a few rather small things that went unnoticed. However, I assume he simply didn't bother acknowledging them.

Arthur's room is on the highest floor of the same building we live in, so we decided to use the elevator to get there. While ascending, I thought we would break it because we stopped two times 'accidentally.' The name of the accident is Roy, by the way. Grace and Memphis didn't seem to like his messing around, but I was almost rolling on the floor laughing.

I knock on the door of Arthur's room. "Come in," comes his voice. I open the door and step in first.

The room – or better to say apartment – is spacious and has panoramic windows that make it look even bigger. The windows overlook the city – Polarium – glowing in the distance. It's dark now, but if my inner compass is right a little to the right of the city, there should be the sharp peaks of the mountain range. And just a small piece of the sea should be visible on the left side of the city. I wish I could have a dwelling with such a view. What does he think of when he looks out of the window?

There isn't much furniture here. A couch with a small table, a desk with a chair, and a small wall of drawers. All in dark colors with minimum details, but so beautiful. To my left, there is a built-in kitchen that matches the room in style. Right in front of me is a door to the big balcony. And one door to the right and two doors to the left, leading to some other rooms.

Arthur stands near the window. Without turning to us, he says, "Is there anything I should know about?"

We keep silent. "I asked a question," he demands, raising his voice just enough to create tension. Not that it wasn't there before.

"No. There's nothing," I say as innocently as possible.

"Really?" He turns sharply. "I doubt that, Lorna. Where have you been?"

"Just walking," I say.

He chuckles. "Walking..." he drawls. "You seem to be doing that a lot. Did you come here to *walk*?" he emphasizes the last word.

"Sorry," says Grace.

"It won't happen again," adds Memphis.

"Or it will," says Roy and I giggle. And Arthur hits Roy in the jaw.

"You two are free to go," Arthur says to Memphis and Grace. They walk out with surprise and worry on their faces.

"So we should just apologize, and that's it?" Roy asks.

"At least," Arthur replies.

"Okay, then. I'm sorry. Really. Memphis won't let me do anything stupid again," Roy says.

"What about you, Lorna?" Arthur asks.

I take a step toward Arthur and look him in the eyes. As I do, a chill runs down my spine, but I say in a low voice, "I won't apologize for something I don't consider myself guilty of."

Arthur looks me in the eyes for a couple more seconds, then his gaze shifts to Roy. "Leave us."

That's it. I'm gonna die... Damn. Was it too stupid of me? Anyway, there's no way back now.

"So what? Now you will kill me?" I spit out.

He puts his hand on my shoulder softly. And in a second, my back hits the wall as he presses me against it. His eyes fixed on mine. He's calm. Deadly calm. "Not now. But be careful, girl.

Bravery and recklessness walk hand in hand. And it's up to you whose steps to follow. Don't choose the wrong path, Rebel." And he lets me go and walks back to the window. I stand there for a couple more seconds, and then I leave, completely stunned.

CHAPTER 9

RECKLESS

Four weeks of training behind. Ten people expelled. It gets harder and harder. But I still hold on. My relationship with Arthur can't get any worse, though.

Rebel... Why does he call me a rebel? I mean, it's obvious. I, Grace, Roy, and Memphis are the only troublemakers here. And I am brave enough to talk back to Arthur every single time. But guys don't have nicknames like I do.

'Bravery and recklessness walk hand in hand. Don't choose the wrong path.' What if I already have?

I walk to the basement floor. It's pretty dark here. Most of the doors are open, and I see people doing things I wasn't expecting them to: drawing, dancing, playing music. That's why they call it the Art Cave, I guess.

Then I see the door labeled 'recording studio.' I stop. Freeze, unable to move. I push on the door gently. It's not locked, but there's no one inside. Only some musical instruments.

An acoustic guitar catches my attention. Without hesitation, I pick it up and start playing. I remember how I played guitar in my room at my mother's house. One of not many things I was allowed to do. And I absolutely loved it.

The guitar feels both familiar and foreign in my hands. It's been so long since I last played that even the marks on my fingers have disappeared. I play some random melodies and hum some tunes and get all warm and cozy inside. I really need to get myself a guitar and get back to songwriting.

In some time, the door opens and two men walk in. "It was great," one of them says.

"Thanks," I say, smiling. "I'm Lorna." I stretch a hand, and he shakes it.

"I'm Ricky, and that's Dan," he points to the other man. I shake his hand, too.

"So, are you musicians?" I ask.

"Do we look like them?" says Ricky, looking at me. He is short with green hair, shoulder length, and tattooed arms, and Dan is much taller than him and has short black hair and bright green eyes.

"Um... yeah," I say. They sigh with relief together.

"We were already afraid that we don't." Dan laughs. "Hey. Do you wanna jam with us? Let's be a band, what do you say?" I am shocked by the out-of-the-blue suggestion, but I agree.

We jam for about an hour before I have to leave. We chatted a lot too. They're really cool. I like it here.

But I came to the Art Cave for a reason, so I find a door that says 'tattoo parlor' and open it. "Hello?"

A girl with dark brown skin and almost black eyes approaches me. Her white-as-snow hair with pink strands looks so bright on her.

"Hey, I'm Skylar. You're new here, aren't you? I'm a tattoo artist."

I tell her about my idea, and she eagerly agrees to take me as a new client. It's easy to see when people are passionate about what they do. I will never not love to witness that.

She gets me in a chair and starts preparing everything. I never got a tattoo before, so I'm a little nervous. I've always wanted to get a few, though, so I'm still extremely excited. I also hate to admit it, but I'm kind of scared it will be unpleasantly painful.

She sits near me and takes my hand. She starts tattooing. It stings a little, but it's more than fine. I completely relax in a few minutes, letting my mind drift.

There are a lot of things in my head. I think too much and get lost in my thoughts easily. I think of my childhood, my dreams and goals, my friends, and just a lot of random shit.

Then, unexpectedly, even for myself, I ask Skylar, "Hey, have you ever been in love?"

"Of course," she says, pointing at another tattoo artist next to us. "That's my girlfriend, Evangeline."

"Oh," I say, "It's nice to have someone near, isn't it?" I look at Evangeline. Her bald head is covered with ink. I understand that her skin is white, but I almost don't see it because of how many tattoos she has.

"Why are you asking?" Skylar says, smiling. I open my mouth to answer, but she interrupts me. "Wait. Let me guess. You have fallen for someone you shouldn't have."

I nod. It's *very* precise. Arthur rarely leaves my head these days. When I don't think of how much I hate him, I think of how much I want him mine.

"Oh, I know that feeling, girl. Maybe this person is not that bad, huh?" She says, hope filling her voice.

"Maybe," I say, "I don't really know him." I stare at the wall.

Weird, huh? To fall for someone you don't know. "And I will never know him. He's not someone who opens up to others," I add.

Suddenly, I realize that if someone knows the inside of Arthur it's his tattoo artist. But I won't dare to ask Skylar. She shouldn't know who my mysterious love interest is. Maybe later I'll confide in her, but not now. And the questioning will be too strange if I don't tell her why I ask.

"It's finished," Skylar says. I look at my fingers and see the fresh ink. It says RECKLESS. I am reckless. And that's ok. That's the choice I've made.

Evangeline comes to us and says, "Hey Sky, Arthur called, wants to get a new tattoo. Are you free already?"

"Yeah," Skylar says. "What's it?"

"Just a word on the forearm. Shouldn't take much time."

"He said which word? Maybe it's something like..." she pauses for a moment. "What if it's something like hippopotomonstrosesquippedaliophobia?"

Evangeline laughs. "Did you just make it up?"

"Nope. It's an existing word. It's the name of the phobia of long words," she says and pretends to adjust her glasses, and that along with their conversation makes me smile.

"Anyway, it's not, uh... that. It's just 'rebel'," the bald-headed girl says and goes back to her workplace.

My heart sinks. Rebel?

"Like he has a spare place," mutters Skylar.

"I should go," I say. "Thank you, Skylar."

"Don't forget to heal it properly," she reminds me and waves me goodbye. I almost run out because I don't wanna accidentally meet with Arthur.

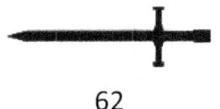

Later that evening, I lie in bed waiting for everyone to fall asleep to sneak out to the gym. Guys already know about my activities, but old habits still stay. I stare at the ceiling, and there's just one thought on my mind. *Why rebel? What does it mean to him?* And how is that connected with how he calls me? Maybe I remind him of someone he once loved and lost? That would make sense, I guess. But if it's so, why does he hate me? Is it because I'm here and whoever he thinks of is not? So many questions and not a single answer. I really want to believe that he just secretly likes me, but I'm not stupid enough to indulge that thought.

CHAPTER 10

I ADMIT

We're fighting again. This time I'm paired with Logan, a middle blond guy. Arthur steps out of the ring and says, "New rules. You fight until one of you is unable to go on. You can start."

For a moment, I hesitate, and Logan hits me in my temple. All of us got visibly less careful with each other. I feel a little dizzy for a second, but keep my balance and kick back. At his stomach. Then ribs and the jaw without a pause. He takes a step back. Then he tries to hit me, but I dodge and hit his leg, sending him to the floor.

Logan gets up and I see that he is determined to, if not kill me, then at least win this fight. He tries to hit my face. I block, but he hits from the other side. Then again, and again while I'm disoriented. My lip is bleeding, and I wipe the blood from it. Then I feel blood on my eyebrow. Fuck that.

I rush at Logan, trying to send him to the ground, but instead he sends me. I manage to dodge his stomp and get up. I punch him in the throat, and he coughs staggering back. Then I go for the ribs and the left temple. He loses his balance, and I use it to grab his arm and twist it. He groans and falls. And doesn't get up.

"Is it all you've got, Logan?" Arthur says. But Logan doesn't respond. Arthur rolls his eyes just for a brief second. "Okay. Next."

At the end of the training, Arthur asks, "So now, who wants to fight me?"

Everyone is still, but I step forward immediately. "Me."

He grins. "Come here, Rebel."

I go to the ring.

"Withstand for 15 minutes," he says.

"Why do you think I won't defeat you faster?" I taunt. I'm not delusional, I know it's a very unlikely scenario, but still.

"Okay, Rebel. Let's see." He tries to hit me, but I block. It won't be like the last time. I know a thing or two now.

One more attempt. And one more. And I hit back. His right side. Then he grabs my arm and throws me to the side. I get up fast, though my leg hurts.

"Now let's get to it." He grins, and in a second I'm on the floor again. He kicks my side. I roll out of the way as he brings his foot down.

I get up once more and manage to deliver a blow to his throat and jaw. Doesn't help much, unfortunately. I land a few more blows to his stomach and face. It makes me happy when I see a small streak of blood on his lip. Damn, he looks even hotter, bleeding. How I want to lick it off him...

My second-long fantasy costs me the air when he hits me right at my sternum. I fall to my knees. He kicks my chin with his knee, and I fall back. I don't waste time as I roll to the other side of the ring to give myself at least a few seconds to breathe.

It's been a while now, the 15 minutes must be over soon. *You can do this,* I say to myself. I'm bleeding in more places than I can count, and my vision blurs with tears that well up in my eyes because of pain. I can't control it. But I hit him again at his side, and he hits me back effortlessly.

Roy shouts, "15 minutes up!" And we stop.

Arthur comes to me and says in a low voice so no one can hear, "That was indeed reckless." For a moment, I catch his eyes on mine.

During my night training today, I don't do much. I can't. It hurts to even move. I lie on the floor thinking about everything that happened here.

After some time, I get up and go to the Art Cave to the recording studio. I take the guitar, a pencil, and a sheet of paper. I just play and write. Feels good to do that again.

In a couple of days, I meet with Ricky and Dan at the studio. I show them my lyrics and instrumentals. We're gonna record it.

Ricky says, "Hey, so we're a band now, right?"

"Kind of," I agree.

"Then we need a bassist. I can ask my brother," says Dan.

"And a name," adds Ricky.

In about half an hour, Dan's brother, Blaze comes. He's neither tall nor short. His hair is long and combed into a ponytail. His eyes are dark brown.

We sit in a circle on the floor trying to invent a name for the band, but everything is bullshit.

"Blood Brothers," says Blaze.

"And a sister," I add sarcastically.

"Damn..."

"Love Bites," suggests Ricky.

"Too cheesy and boring," says Blaze, and they start fighting jokingly. It doesn't escape my attention that their movements aren't sloppy. At least basic training must be mandatory for everyone here.

"A name doesn't have to be vampire-themed, you know," says Dan. "Just saying. Imagine if humans called their bands something like Pizza Sisters or some shit."

I laugh. "It sounds pretty cool, actually."

I look at the guys fighting, and insight comes to me, and I say, "What about Rebels?"

"I like that," says Blaze.

"Isn't that too cheesy?" Dan laughs at him.

"That's cool," interrupts Ricky. "We need to get this tattooed," he adds, and we go to the tattoo parlor.

Along with *REBELS* on my left forearm, I got *art* surrounded by a heart on my wrist. It's an act of honesty, admission. I won't hide my feelings for him from myself anymore. And others can think that I just like art, which is actually true too.

CHAPTER 11

DONE WHAT I COULD

I stand in front of the mirror and look at myself. I only have my underwear on me. My dark blue – almost black – hair covers my bare shoulders. My hands, parts of my chest and stomach are now covered with tattoos – I seem to visit Skylar rather often. The only thing that's left of the old me is my eyes. They are still grey. But the look is different, anyway. I am a completely different person, both outside and inside.

Almost two months of training went by. Hundreds of fights won and lost. Thousands of hours of work. Millions of scratches and bruises. Day after day, week after week, we woke up at 5 a.m., went to the gym at 6, and had like 10 hours of training. 12 people have already left. Only 11 stayed. And today... today is the day that will determine our fate and our future. The day of the test. Those who fail leave. And those who succeed can stay and finally be turned.

We are gathered outdoors on a balcony, near some area surrounded by a high fence. It's made of stone, but one segment is metal and looks movable, probably a gate. Arthur told us that we would have to complete an obstacle course before the said gate closes.

"I'll show you what you have to do first," Arthur says and goes to the fence. He sets the timer – 10 minutes – and he starts the race.

He moves so smoothly, like it's not harder for him than walking. Well, probably it is true. *Come on, Lorna, you have to focus on the task, not him.*

First, we have to run, then jump, then again run, then shoot... Damn. How the fuck am I supposed to remember everything? The gate is going to close after the time is up, regardless of whether we do what we have to or not. Arthur finishes in four minutes and I can't help but be jealous of such a result. When — if — I'm a vampire, my physical abilities will increase too, but it'll still take years of training to be that good.

Roy is the first to try. He manages it just before the gate closes. He looks completely out of breath and strength.

One by one, Arthur calls us, and we hear *'You stay'* or *'You leave.'* I shiver at the thought I can not be on time. I don't know what I will do then. The two of us already couldn't make it. I feel genuinely sorry for them. All of us became good friends, and all worked really hard. It seems unfair that one impossibly difficult test decides everything in a matter of 10 minutes.

"Lorna." I hear my name and take a deep breath. I am the last one. I have to calm down.

I climb down the stairs and go to the gate. Arthur sets the timer, and I hear a signal and start running.

After running for about two minutes, I'm not tired yet, so I try to run faster. I glance at the timer on the wall. Three minutes now.

I have to climb a wall. I go up pretty fast. I cut my arm slightly off a rock, but it's not a big deal. I barely even notice. Then I get down just as uneventfully. 5 minutes.

Now shooting, I remind myself. I take a gun. One shot, two, three. I don't miss a single target.

Now knife throwing. One by one I let five knives fly and they all lodge perfectly in their targets. Success. My night training sessions paid off, and I feel insanely proud of myself. 6:30.

Now running with obstacles. A few meters in, and I dodge some pendulum shit. I keep running and slide under a barrier. Then jump over a few other ones. I run further and almost trip over my own leg. I keep my balance and dodge one more time. Done.

The finish line. Time's almost up. I run as fast as I can. 9:40.

Faster. I'm almost out of breath, my lungs burn. 9:50.

I feel every muscle in my body. I'm almost there. 9:55.

And then the gate closes. I'm late. Just 10 more meters and I would've made it. I cover the distance in no time. But what for?

The heat rushes to my face. I can't give up now. Not after what I've been through.

I should climb over the fence.

The gate is made of sleek metal, there's no way I can climb that. But the walls are made of stones. So I rush to the wall immediately.

I start my climb. The stones are way sharper than they look, and they cut my hands badly. But I swallow the pain and climb. My hands reach the top of the wall, and I pull myself up. I swing my legs over, look down for a second, and just jump. To my surprise, I land quite successfully with a roll and stand up.

Now I'm ready to hear *'You leave'*, hug my friends, and go, even though I have no idea where. At least I've done everything I could.

I look at Grace and see tears in her eyes. I almost cry myself. But I bite my lip instead. I can't cry. Not in front of everyone. I just can't.

And then I hear, "You stay." What? How? I failed. I mean... I did. I know it. Damn... Come on, it can't be true. But well, I won't argue.

Arthur announces that in the evening we'll be turned. Finally. I can't believe I've made it. During the announcement, I just stand in complete shock.

We go to our rooms, and as soon as we enter, Grace says, "I thought he wouldn't let you join. You actually failed it, you... you weren't in time." She hugs me tightly, and I return the hug.

"I know that, I'm shocked myself, I can't believe it, it's so strange," I rush out. "You know, it's not like him to be kind or that sort of thing. And I'm not the best here. And damn, some did better than me and just were late, and he said goodbye so easily. I don't understand his logic, but, well, about that, I won't argue for sure."

Memphis laughs and says, "Wow, come on, we've found a topic that you won't argue with Arthur about!" We all laugh.

"There should be something," I say.

CHAPTER 12

VAMPIRE

At 10 p.m., we all stand together at the gym, waiting to be turned. Arthur comes to us and says, "Today you'll join the army. Already as vampires. After the turning, there will be no way back, so if you want to leave, it's your last chance to get out alive."

Everyone stands still. Until one girl just goes to the door. Jess. Why? She wanted this so much.

I steal a glance at Roy. I know he's in love with her. It must hurt so much to see someone you like just leave, knowing you most likely won't see them again.

And then he runs after her. *No, please, I don't want to lose him.* I don't want to lose any of my friends. He catches her hand and says something to her. I can't hear what and the wait is overwhelming. *Please stay.*

In a minute, Arthur says, "You two, decide. Either go or stay."

Roy turns to look at all of us standing there, and he looks completely lost. I know he wouldn't want her to go, but is it bad enough for him to leave with her? I hold my breath. *Please.*

He takes a step back from her and returns to the line. I sigh with relief. I mean, I'm sorry for him, I really am. Probably I'm more selfish than I thought.

"Anyone else?" Arthur asks. This time, everyone stays.

Now finally, this moment, the turning.

To turn a human into a vampire, the latter has to bite a human – most commonly, it's the neck. Then a vampire bites themselves – usually the wrist – and presses their wound to that of a human so that the blood can mix. I'm pretty sure you can do it less dramatically, but vampires seem to love sticking to useless rituals and traditions. I find it kinda cool too, actually. And the final step is for a human to drink the blood of their maker.

Memphis is the first, and I turn left to look at him. My heart starts beating a little too fast for my comfort, and I close my eyes for a moment, taking a deep breath.

After 3 more people, it's my turn. Arthur comes to me and I remove my hair from my neck, not meeting his eyes. Gotta admit I'm a little nervous.

Arthur puts his hand on the side of my neck to keep me still and sinks his fangs into me. I was mentally prepared for the pain, but it doesn't hurt at all, it's even pleasant. Although I don't know, maybe it's just because it's Arthur. He's so close I can smell him. A barely noticeable trace of perfume and probably a bit of shampoo or soap. I want to dig my hands into his hair and lose myself in his scent.

When he starts pulling away, he brushes my neck with his lips. I feel his hot breath on my skin. *Is it supposed to be like that?* I'm not sure. Or maybe I'm just crazy. I have to stop thinking about him. I have to stop thinking something can happen between us. He's my leader now. Moreover, he very likely hates me.

Then he looks me in the eyes. It's less than a second, but these milliseconds are now stuck in my head. His gaze, so determined and powerful – the gaze that seems to drill a hole through me right to the bone. And it's so cold. I almost shiver.

He bites his wrist – reopening the wounds left from other turnings – and presses his hand to my neck. Then he offers me his hand, and I drink blood for the first time in my life.

The very second my lips touch his hand, I feel some kind of energy within me. It's clear that something has changed, and it has changed forever. I'm not human. Not anymore. I can feel it.

The blood swirls on my tongue, its salty taste seems rather good now. I swallow, and I can almost feel it travel through me. It's such a weird feeling.

I feel like everything goes numb and the world around me fades. But at the same time, I feel more alert. I hear every rustle, every smell, every damn thing. It's overwhelming.

I pull away. Or rather, Arthur pulls his hand away. It was magical. I will never forget that moment.

Arthur turns everyone else – the time barely enough for me to come from the high of just being turned – and goes to the center of the room and says, "Congratulations to you all. Welcome to the army. Today, you can go and relax. Tomorrow in the evening, we'll have the ball to celebrate newcomers. It's an ancient tradition we have. Tomorrow, you also won't have a training session, since your bodies need time to fully transform. *However*, the fact that you're in the army now does not mean that your training is over. You still have too many things to learn."

He gives us some instructions on how to go through the turning. And what to do after our bodies transform. These are some insane changes, so a little guidance is definitely appreciated.

Grace comes to me and hugs me tightly. "We made it! Can you believe it?"

"No, I really can't," I say, smiling. "Come on, I was the worst trainee at the beginning, and still, I'm here." I smile even broader. I fucking made it.

There are 8 of us who stayed: me, Grace, Roy, Memphis, Ruby, Abigail, Randy, and Logan. Our small unbreakable team.

CHAPTER 13

YOU'RE WORTH IT, REBEL

Today, we all prepare for the ball. What to wear, make-up, hairstyle, shoes? Damn... it's hard. After almost half a day of thinking, I finally decided, though. I go to the dressing room. Yeah, they have a freaking dressing room here. Insane.

The girl who works here – Maria – is very nice and looks heavenly with her short white hair and sky-blue eyes. She helped me with everything, and we have just finished. What I see in the mirror is absolutely amazing. Maria is something!

I've chosen a black dress. It has a leather corset top part and a silk skirt that isn't tight but not fluffy either, the fabric just falls down naturally. It is long on the back and short on the front. The neckline is deep, triangle form. It reveals the middle of my chest and goes down just a little more. My arms are bare, so all of my tattoos are on display. My heels – also black – are closed and almost reach my knees.

I left my hair to fall loose on my shoulders – like I do most of the time when I'm not training – and just added a little volume.

My make-up of choice is blood red lipstick, black eye shadow, and eyeliner. If my mom could see me now, she'd never recognize me, which is definitely a good thing.

And I'm already late. So I thank Maria and run towards the ballroom. I've memorized all the important places here already, so now this behemoth of a building doesn't feel like a labyrinth anymore.

When I enter, I immediately notice Grace across the room and head to her. When she sees me, she says, "Wow, Lorna, you look so cool. Are you going to a gothic party after the ball?" She laughs and hugs me.

Suddenly, I realize how funny we probably look together. Her dress is like a princess dress. I don't know how this color is called, but it is something between pink and beige. The dress has some kind of lace, and it looks very gentle. And it suits her. It really does. I know she likes that kind of things. Nice, soft-colored, and pretty. I am the complete opposite. I like black clothes, tattoos, and all that stuff. Maybe they're right when they say that opposites attract after all.

I let my gaze roam around the ballroom. It's spacious and, while made in darker colors, it doesn't create a dark atmosphere. The high ceilings are adorned with gothic chandeliers, their lightbulbs resembling candles.

Along the perimeter, red and black sofas are full of exquisitely dressed people. I notice a few of my friends and take a mental note to go greet them later.

My gaze lands on the other side of the room, on Arthur with his friend Damian, a leader of another clan. At first, I almost didn't recognize Arthur because of how he looks. *He looks absolutely amazing,* the thought invades my mind. *Ah, that's not the direction I was going to go with that initial thought,* I tell myself. *Well, I mean it, but... fuck.* I can't even gather my thoughts when I look at him.

He looks rather unusual today, he is wearing a black suit that suits and fits him perfectly, a white shirt, and a black tie. His hair is combed back and doesn't fall on his face the way it always does. He looks extremely classy except for his tattooed hands and neck, and perfectly done eyeliner, and just a little of black eyeshadow. The blue of his eyes looks even brighter with the make-up.

For a minute or two, I just stare at him. There's something in him – except for his hotness – that makes me want to drown in him. I'm not just attracted to him physically. My soul is attracted to him too, and I absolutely can't explain why.

A girl joins them. She wears a long grey dress that is literally glowing because of the sequins that are on it. She is incredibly beautiful. Her long silver blond hair with black strands falls in waves to her waist. Her skin is almost snow white. I wonder who she is.

"Lorna," Grace says, pulling at my hand, "are you there?"

"Yeah... yes, sure, I was just thinking."

"You are strange." She laughs and looks in the direction I was staring. "I think someone lied at the girls' night." She grins. I just roll my eyes.

Ruby and Abigail joined me and Grace so now we all dance together to the loud music.

"Can you believe where we are, Lorna?" Ruby shouts to me.

"Hell no," I reply. "I mean, especially not you. Heels Ruby, seriously?" I say, remembering the first training session. No one ever mentioned this episode, but I decide it's too funny to just let it slide.

"I came here to find a boyfriend, you know," she retorts.

"And now you're a soldier in a vampire army and still single," Abigail taunts as she flips her shoulder-length curly blond hair back in a dramatic gesture. I burst into laughter at that.

"At least I'm not dreaming of spending a night with Arthur," Ruby replies.

"Ooo, that was personal," I say.

Right on cue, Memphis and Logan join us and Grace doesn't miss a chance to brag about finding her love by saying "Well, you find it when you least expect it" and kissing Memphis on a cheek.

"I never knew you were such a show-off," I say and she laughs.

We keep dancing until the host announces the slow dance. Logan immediately invites Abigail, and Ruby excuses herself and runs to some guy I've never seen before.

I go to the bar and decide to wait there until it's over. Grace and Memphis sure need some privacy as well. By the way, where's Roy? I haven't seen him yet. Maybe if he were here, I'd dance with him. However, it would be weird. Everyone would think that we're dating. I laugh to myself. Picturing us as a couple is really crazy.

At the bar, I order a drink. Alcohol doesn't have any effect on vampires, so now I can drink whatever I want with no consequences at all.

I take it and start to walk a little away from the bar stand. *Bam!* I bump into someone and spill my drink on them. I lift my eyes. It's her. The girl that was with Arthur and Damian.

"Oh my god, I'm so sorry. I didn't mean to. I didn't see you," I rash out. Her unearthly beauty makes me even more nervous than I would normally be after spilling my drink on someone.

"Oh, it's ok." She smiles. "Don't worry, I'm fine. It's just a cocktail. Not the first time, not the last." She pauses before saying, "I'm Iris, by the way." Why would you introduce yourself to someone after meeting them like this? She seems *really* nice, and her voice is charming. Her pale blue eyes search my face.

"I'm Lorna," I say, embarrassed.

"Nice to meet you, Lorna. So... I guess I'll see you around. Have a nice evening," she says casually, as if I didn't spill the whole drink on her magical dress.

"You too," I say. Well, she *is* nice. Damn, so awkward.

Why am I so clumsy? Okay, whatever. I'll just stand here and wait until this fucking slow dance is over before I mess something up again.

The music only now starts playing, and more couples appear on the dancefloor. I sit alone at the bar, just watching them. I could use a dance too, but well, the only person I am interested in would never ever invite me. And I would never dare to invite him. I know he hates me, so I lower my head and stare at my feet, silently begging the song to finish faster.

Then I see a hand right in front of me, and a familiar voice says, "Can I have this dance?" I almost choke on air as I realize the voice belongs to Arthur.

"Yeah, uh... why not... okay," I stutter out as I lift my head. I'm too surprised and too nervous to answer normally.

I take his hand, and he leads me to the dancefloor. When we're almost in the middle, he pulls me a little closer to him and puts his hand on my waist. I hold my breath.

We're not even friends, but I feel calm with him, even though I know his unstable personality. Am I crazy? I must be.

I feel his warm body against mine. Now I wish the song lasted forever. We sway to the rhythm together, and I hold his hand in mine. His skin is so smooth I would never believe the hand in mine belongs to a warrior if I didn't know it for a fact. It takes all the concentration I've got to keep my own hand from trembling.

I look to the side because I don't wanna meet his gaze. And I notice Grace's at first surprised face, and then she gives me that oh-I-knew-I-was-right look. I wish I didn't look at her either. So for the rest of the dance, I just stare at the black wall behind Arthur's back.

The music stops too soon, and Arthur says, "Thank you for the dance. By the way, you look gorgeous. Have a nice night." He turns on his heels and leaves the room.

The dance has just finished, but I don't remember what music was playing, don't remember what was going on around us. All I can think of is that those were the precious minutes I spent with him. Those minutes that will probably never happen again.

I go to sit near the bar once more, just trying to take it all in. Iris comes to me bringing Damian along – his slightly tanned skin with a few intricate tattoos looks deep brown next to hers.

"Hey, Lorna. That's Damian, my boyfriend. D, that's Lorna."

"Nice to meet you," I say and extend my hand. He shakes it eagerly.

"Nice to meet you, too. Do you like the ball?" he asks kind of formally, fixing his bluish-grey eyes on mine.

"Yes, it's amazing," I answer honestly. "All these clothes, dances... it's wonderful."

"Yeah, I love it too," Iris says. "Wanna have a drink with us?"

"Can't say no to that," I agree.

While we were having a drink, I didn't notice that an hour passed. Damian and Iris are such lovely people, and we were just talking and talking about everything in the world. It feels like we've known each other forever. That was an extremely nice conversation, and the only question that was on my mind the whole time was, *How can a man like Damian be friends with someone like my favorite Mr. Black?* Like... they're just so different. Damian is such a gentleman, he's polite, tactful, nice, and so on. And Arthur... well... I sigh internally.

Finally, I can't hold back and ask, "Damian, how long have you known Arthur?"

"Oh, feels like forever. Which, for you, is actually true, I guess." He smiles. "We met during the war, in the middle of a battle. Those were rough times for everyone. He saved my life."

"What happened?" I ask and then add, "Of course, if you don't mind telling."

"Of course, I don't," he says. "Though Arthur wouldn't want me to say it. He is not someone who likes to reminisce about the past. Anyway, I was only 25 then. Just a child thrown into the harsh world of the war. All I could do was try to survive. Once I got caught by the enemy soldiers. I don't know if they wanted to kill or imprison me, which in my case would've meant certain death, anyway. When they were dragging me somewhere through the battlefield, Arthur noticed us, and he saved me, even though for him back then I was just a kid who went for a walk at the wrong hour to the wrong place." He laughs warmly.

"Then we met a couple of decades later. Again at war, but that time I was already a soldier. We were on the same side, and gradually we became friends. He is my closest one still. He's like a brother to me. Many things I know now I learned from him," he states.

"Wow," I say. "You know, I think you do have a story worth telling." Living for so long, fighting for your life so many times. It indeed makes a person interesting.

Iris and Damian leave somewhere, and I decide that I need some fresh air. Through the long corridors – usually dark at this hour, but tonight filled with lights – I go to the staircase, which leads to the balcony. I like the view there, it's my favorite place in the castle. The balcony is almost at the top of it – the only thing higher is Arthur's apartment.

I go to stand by the railing and stare at the city lights in the distance. I close my eyes for a moment and imagine I'm on the top of a mountain and below me is the stormy sea. I let go of the railing and smile to myself.

When I finally open my eyes, the peace I just felt is replaced with unease. The thoughts about what happened and what's gonna happen invade my mind instantly.

I hear footsteps behind my back. I turn and see a familiar figure.

"Decided to use a break, huh?"

"Yeah," I say, "you know, just some fresh air, new thoughts, and a beautiful view."

"Yeah, I got the idea," he cuts me off sharply.

He looks even more beautiful in the moonlight. Arthur is standing next to me in less than a meter distance. I can hear his breath, pulse, and heartbeat. Somehow, it is magical to me. My enhanced senses don't make it any easier, either. And then I remember the question that didn't leave me all day. "Why did you let me join the army?"

He chuckles. "I was waiting for this question." He pauses. "Because you're worth it, Rebel. And you deserve it."

"But I failed, right? I wasn't in time," I counter. "I didn't go through the gate, and that was the task. And I did not cope with it."

"You didn't give up, though," he points out. "You know, being in time is just about your physical abilities, and what *you've* done shows that maybe you're not the best in technique... However, if we compare what you are now and what you were when you came here, that's a universal difference..." he trails off, thinking. "And you were the only one who trained over time, right?" he adds, glancing at me, and I look at him, confused.

He grins and says, "Come on, you really think I don't know about your night training sessions?"

For whatever reason, I feel a little embarrassed.

"I appreciate it, you know. That's what I call being determined," he continues. "To not give up. Never. That's what you have in yourself. Others don't. You didn't give up and climbed the fucking fence, cut your arms. It's worth respect," he states. "You know, to be honest, in a battle, I would rather rely on you than on someone who was in time." Worth respect? Rely on me? Is he really telling me this?

"Thanks, I... I appreciate what you said," I reply.

"Don't be confused. It's not that I like you." He smiles a little. "Still, I believe one day you'll become one of the best warriors ever."

His eyes fix on mine, but this time there's no cold in them. They're still as blue as the sky. I'm still drowning in them. But this time I'm not drowning in the ice. They're warm.

I'm into him. *Really* into him. I have to admit that fully.

I love him, I do. I want him to be mine, and I want to be his. I want to look into these eyes for hours every single day.

"Thanks," I say again, though I don't believe his words. I'm not sure I can be a very good warrior, let alone the best one. But I'll do what I can, that's for sure.

Suddenly, I say, "I won't let you down." He nods and then leaves.

I decide not to go back to the ball and go to bed right after.

CHAPTER 14

I'LL MISS IT

Next day I wake up, get dressed, and go to the gym. I wonder what it will be now that we're actually in the army and vampires.

When Arthur comes, he says, "Now you are in my army, which means that you were somehow better than others. But it doesn't mean you are the best, you are not. Your bodies still need time to rebuild from humans to vampires, so today there won't be a training session. Instead, you can use that time to move to your new rooms. Eric," he points to the man who came with him, "will show you."

Eric – who I first thought to be our instructor – smiles at us. It's so good to see someone being nice. It makes me feel like I'm at my place, and some people are actually happy to see us here.

We got an hour to take our stuff and move out of our rooms, and now it's time to leave.

At the door, I suddenly feel an ache in my chest. It's like I'm leaving a place that is really dear to me. The bed I used to lie in, waiting for everyone to fall asleep, thinking of everything in the world, the window through which I could barely see the sky but the tiniest sight of it made me feel like I could make it, the mirror I used to look in and see how I was changing… I'll miss it. I glance at the room for the last time and leave to catch up with the others.

Eric is waiting for us outside the main building. When we're all here, he starts walking towards the other building. I don't want to think about my old apartment, so I catch up with him to talk.

"Hey," I stretch my hand, "I'm-"

"Lorna," he finishes for me and shakes my hand and I notice a traditional rose tattoo on his. "I know."

"How come you know me?" I ask, confused.

"Arthur mentioned you," he answers.

"Seems like you have a good relationship," I point out.

"As good as you can have with Arthur." He laughs. "I heard you didn't succeed in it." He giggles teasingly and adds, "He's not that bad if you get to know him better." I want to ask something else, but we're at the spot.

The building in front of us is made of stone, gothic style, but it's much smaller than the main one. Eric stops right in front of the door and assigns each of us a room. Mine is on the fifth floor, room 11.

When I get there, I push the door open and see a simple room with just one bed in it. Bare walls and no other furniture. Eric mentioned that we would have to decorate our rooms ourselves. I like that. I can make everything the way I want it.

I walk into the kitchen, which already has everything needed. So does the bathroom. Both are made in light colors and it makes me roll my eyes. I'll have to correct that little mistake of whoever decorated that room.

I sit on the bed, thinking about how I can improve my living space without having many resources. I decide to go to the Art Cave to find something interesting for my room. I'm sure I will.

Right before I leave, I see an envelope on the kitchen table. I didn't notice it before. When I lift it to examine closer, I realize it's too heavy for an envelope and pretty thick as well. I open it and see a communicator and the note that says, 'Now that you *are a part of the clan, you should have a means of communication.'*

I take the communicator, and it feels weird in my hands. Even though I've held one before, it definitely wasn't that fancy. This place *does* have the best possible equipment.

I turn the communicator – *my* communicator – on. It vibrates with a message. It's from a group chat for the eight of us and Arthur. The text from Arthur says, *'Communicators are delicate, please don't drop it,'* followed by a weird winking face. Arthur really can't miss an opportunity to tease us. The chat is probably so we can receive information from him. And an overtime dose of his sarcasm.

My communicator buzzes in my hands again. Another chat, this time just the eight of us. And the first message is from Roy, *'I think we'll feel better without Arthur in our chat. So, who wants to party tonight?'* Typical Roy.

I put the communicator in my pocket – obviously careful not to drop it, as instructed – and leave the room.

At the Art Cave, I go to the tattoo parlor. When I enter, Skylar is there.

"Hi, how are you?" she says.

"I'm fine, just moved to the new room. Officially part of the clan now." I smile.

"Oh, congratulations!" she says and hugs me. I hug her back.

"I actually came to ask if you know someone who can have something that may help me to like... move faster," I stutter. And then the thought hits my mind. "On second thought, do you have paints?"

She is surprised but says, "I know someone who does, wait a minute."

In a couple of minutes, she returns with paint sprays. I thank her and rush out.

Art Cave is a treasure. I've found so many useful things and met quite a few nice people. Some random guy and a girl even managed to find me an old fancy wardrobe. *And* they helped me to move it into my room.

I start renovating. First, I paint the walls chaotically with different colors on the black base. As I do, the paint drips on the floor and I'm instantly very happy I found a carpet to cover all that mess.

I cover my bed with black and green sheets and move it to the corner of the room, right next to the window.

I put a garland with lights on a wall right below the ceiling and move the table from the kitchen to the main room. I stand in the middle of my room thinking, *well, now that's really mine.*

I hear a knock on my door and open it. I see Dan and Blaze.

"Heeey!" Dan shouts and hugs me. "Congratulations, soldier. We have something for you." He shoves me an acoustic guitar. It looks like green marble and is almost glowing. I look at it in awe.

"So what are you waiting for? Try it," says Blaze.

"Thanks," I breathe out and take the instrument. I sit on the floor near the window, tune the guitar a little, and start playing. It sounds so good, and I already feel that I'm bonding with it. My new love. Arthur can wait.

"What do you think about playing at the party tonight?" asks Blaze.

"Party?" I ask, looking up at him as he sits on my bed.

"Yeah, this crazy kid... what's his name?" He clicks his fingers, trying to remember. "Roy. He organizes some shit. I like you youngsters because you never bore. So what do ya think?"

I giggle. I didn't realize Roy would go to that extent with his party threats. But I agree to play.

CHAPTER 15

ALL SAID OUT LOUD

I have time before the party, so I decided to visit Maria so that she can help me with my look. I need something absolutely *stunning*. It will be my debut as a musician after all.

I wear a leather jacket, black jeans and a crop top, heeled combat boots and a massive choker. My hair is combed to one side.

While Maria does my make-up – eyeliner and black lipstick – she asks me if I liked the welcoming ball. I tell her that it was awesome, about meeting Iris and Damian and the fun I had with my friends. And then she asks me the question I feared the most. About my slow dance. She asks if I danced with someone.

"Yeah, I did," I say, trying to steady my breathing. My memories fly to that dance.

"You know," I say, unable to hold it back anymore, "the guy I danced with... I think I might be in love with him." I pause. "No, I'm sure I'm in love with him. And..." I try to shape my thoughts so I don't sound like an idiot. "I think that first of all, he hates me and he's not good for me. He's not good for me," I repeat. I'm trying to convince myself again. I thought I was over it.

"Who is that guy?" she asks. "Do I know him?"

I hesitate. I thought I admitted my feelings to myself, but saying it out loud means to *actually* admit and embrace them.

"Arthur," I finally say, quietly, but she hears. I feel like my body is burning.

"You mean..." Maria trails off.

"Yeah," I say, not letting her finish.

I look in the mirror at her reflection. She's obviously a little confused, but it doesn't look like she thinks I'm crazy. Maybe I'm not? I mean, I'm definitely not the first girl who's charmed by him.

"You're his type," she says finally.

I raise my eyebrows at her. "What do you mean? What's the 'type'?"

"Brave, strong, smart, extraordinary. A little crazy," she says with a laugh.

I bite my lip and smile, "I wish you were right." Is she? Maybe I know Arthur much less than I thought. "Why do you even think I'm all those things?"

"I'm rather good at reading people. And we've talked about a few things. And I've heard about your exam. Impressive really."

Wow, I really did pull some crazy shit out there, apparently. "Thank you," I say.

Later I'm in the Art Cave club. It's a dark room filled with colorful lights and a stage at the front. I notice Grace and Memphis and come to them.

"Ooo," howls Grace when she sees me. "Who are you impressing tonight?"

I shake my head and laugh. "No one and everyone." Stupid answer.

For a while, we just dance and chat.

"Where is Roy again?" I ask. "If I didn't know better, I'd assume he deliberately avoids all parties."

"No idea," says Memphis. "But I mean, he organized all this, so makes sense if he's busy."

The music stops, and right on cue, I hear Roy's voice. "Hello, everyone. I'm glad you came." He'd make a good host, I think. Charismatic, well-spoken, funny.

While he talks, Dan comes to me and says, "We're opening. Time to go."

I glance at Grace's surprised face, wink at her, and leave with Dan.

We get backstage, where Ricky and Blaze wait. Roy says, "Now ladies and gentlemen, REBELS!" He bows playfully.

We get on stage. Ricky sits at the drums. Dan takes the guitar and Blaze takes the bass. I go to the mic. I say, "Hey everyone! We're REBELS, and tonight we're gonna make you remember us for the rest of your lives. Can only hope the memory will be a good one."

The guys start playing, and I jump to the rhythm, trying to make everyone do the same. I barely see the crowd because of how bright the lights that shine on us are, but I notice the silhouettes start to move and the energy overwhelms me immediately.

I start singing – it's the song I wrote about being who you are and never giving up. I run around the stage, jump, and headbang so hard that by the end of the song I'm exhausted. Everyone cheers.

I look at the crowd. "Want one more song?" I ask, and they cheer louder. I smile at my bandmates and we play a few more.

When we're done, the guys come to me, and we hug each other, bowing. I look at Ricky to my right and Blaze and Dan to my left and smile. I'm at my place. I know it.

Later that night, I walk to my room, humming our songs. In the hallway, I meet Arthur. He stops and asks, "How was the party?"

His gaze travels from my toes to my eyes. I don't really know how to understand his look. He's not looking at me like he did when I talked back, he doesn't look like he wants to kill me. Doesn't look like men look at women when they see us as objects to fuck. His look is more curious, like the look a child gives every new thing, like they want to know what it is. Like he wants to know me. Like he tries to look into me, at my soul, to find out what I'm made of. "Heard you impressed everyone, Rebel."

"It's actually *REBELS*," I comment sarcastically. "Plural. The name of my band," I clarify as coldly as possible.

He smiles with just the corner of his mouth. The way he usually does when I talk back to him, the smile is just a little less predatory this time. "I wasn't talking about the band. I was talking about you."

I stare at him for a moment.

"Anyway. Have a good night," he says and keeps walking.

I turn and open my mouth like I want to say something else. But I don't really know what.

CHAPTER 16

THE GAME

The next day we're gathered at the gym, sleepy from partying all night. Arthur told us the training would be special today, but that didn't stop us.

Arthur enters the gym with Damian on his heels. The former is dressed differently today. He wears a leather jacket instead of his signature cape and a grey t-shirt instead of his usual black. And there's a gun sling attached to his jeans. A gun in it.

"Today," he says, "we'll play a game. That's Damian, a leader of another clan, an ally, and a good friend." Damian smiles. "We're going to have a competition. Our clan against theirs." He points at his friend. "Follow us."

We go outside and leave the castle's territory. Through the woods we go to a fence, a simple metal one with a gate in it. We go inside, where people from Damian's clan are already waiting.

The rules for the game, competition, whatever are rather simple. Each team has its own 'base' where we can plan our actions. Then there is a tower somewhere in the surrounded territory. At the top of the tower, there's a button that makes the tower bells ring. The team that gets to the button first wins.

When we get to our base, Arthur hands each of us a gun. With real bullets. Human bullets.

Good thing you can't kill a vampire with a usual bullet — only silver ones work — so we'll stay alive. However, these bullets can still hurt us. Even though vampires heal fast, it's not fast enough not to notice that you have been shot.

"So, what do we do?" asks Logan, scratching his blonde head and looking at Arthur.

"It's your game, not mine. I've played it hundreds of times. Your turn," he says with his usual indifference.

"Why don't we just go and push this button?" suggests Roy.

"Wow! How logical! How come I didn't think of it?!" says Abigail sarcastically.

"Damian's people might be more experienced than us, we don't even know them. We don't have a chance if we just *go there*," I say with an eye roll.

"You're right," says Grace. "We need a solid plan."

After a couple of minutes, we actually invent a plan. Then we hear a siren – the beginning of the game – and run to our positions.

Me, Randy, and Abigail have the left side to check and move through. The most peaceful one probably because Damian's base is on the right side. However, I still hold my gun ready. Just in case.

Memphis, Roy, and Ruby have the middle. And Grace, Logan, and Arthur have the left. Sending Arthur to basically Damian's side was my idea, which he didn't like. I got it right and clear when he started muttering something about how we're supposed to play the game and not him.

I hear a crack and stop. "Hear this?" I whisper.

Randy goes behind the heavy bushes to check, and we hear a shot and a scream. Me and Abigail share a glance.

A guy comes at us, and I shoot his right shoulder, and he drops the gun. I have a good aim now. Every time I shoot, I feel proud. I rush to the guy and hit him in the jaw and then his shoulder. He answers with a punch to my temple, which makes me feel a little dizzy for a moment. He manages to kick my leg, and I fall. I grab my gun and fire at his ribs twice. He falls, writhing in pain.

Abigail has already helped Randy, who now has a wound in his thigh, and we are ready to go further.

We approach the area without woods, and I see the tower. The bells haven't rung yet. I see the other group: Memphis and Ruby. They went with Roy. Where's he? Memphis is bleeding badly, he's leaning on Ruby to stand on his feet.

At the meadow, I see Logan and Grace fight Damian's people. They need help, so we rush to them.

Arthur and Damian are nowhere to be seen. I'm not so sure about Damian, but something tells me Arthur just opted out somewhere in the middle of the way here. *'It's your game, not mine.'* Asshole.

All around me are people punching and shooting each other. It doesn't really look like a game to me. And then I see one of Damian's people near the tower entrance. We're losing.

I lose my focus on the opponent for a second, and she hits me in the face so hard I fall.

Suddenly, a feeling that I absolutely *need* to do something washes over me. We have to win. I take the gun out of my holster and I shoot my opponent in the jaw – she screams in pain – get up and run towards the tower. I don't like hurting people, but now I don't see any other way to get through, sorry.

Bullets fly past me, and one hits my arm. I don't stop. Then another one hits my stomach, and I fall. Tears well up in my eyes. Being a vampire doesn't make it less painful, but I get up. I can't stop. Not now.

I feel like I felt during the test. And an idea comes to my mind.

I can't outrun the girl that just entered the building. But I can climb a wall, so she doesn't even know I'm going after her. The tower is not too tall, and the walls aren't smooth.

I finally get to the tower and start climbing. It appears to be pretty easy, I would even enjoy it if every move didn't hurt. I climb to one of the windows and break the glass – not sure it was allowed though – and get inside. Now my hand is bleeding. I snort. Fuck the hand, I'm bleeding *everywhere*.

I see the girl right behind me and start running up. She has a gun and fires at me, but I dodge.

I get to the roof and almost push the button when a bullet hits my back and then my leg. I fall with a whimper and hear the girl laugh. Bitch.

She walks to the button triumphantly, but I grab her leg and pull. She falls next to me. Without getting up, I punch her with my unharmed leg, and her gun flies to the side. I punch her temple.

I try to get up even though my body burns with pain. I half crawl to the button and push twice – as agreed to indicate our team. The bells ring once and then again – the sound actually beautiful – and I hear my team cheer.

For a moment, I fall back on the floor and rest my head against the stone. I let out a breath and slowly get up.

I go down the stairs and feel my legs going limp. I don't feel good. Come on, who would after being shot like 5 times? When I walk through the door, I see my teammates smile, shout, and clap their hands. I try to smile in return, and it goes weak. My vision starts to blur. It seems the world around me floats.

Through the dizziness, I see a figure approaching me. It looks like Randy.

I fall, and he catches me in his arms. I black out.

I open my eyes and see a white wall. I'm at the hospital. *Again.*

I rise on my elbows at first and then sit on the bed. My whole body hurts, but I feel better than before. Some of my wounds have already healed themselves. Perks of being a vampire. I get up and go to the door. I have *no desire* to stay here.

I open the door and come face-to-face with the doctor. "Where do you think you're going?" she says in her 'incredibly charming' manner.

"Out," I say. "Let me?"

"You have to stay here. Your injuries are pretty serious," she says.

"I'll live. Don't worry," I say.

"I am the doctor here, and I do not allow you to leave yet. You have to fully recover."

"Like I'm asking for your permission," I snap and leave.

It's not like I'm actually fine, but staying here won't do me any good. I head towards the exit and see Arthur entering the building. When I walk past him, he grabs my arm, and I stop. I keep looking in the direction where I was going, not paying attention to him.

In my peripherals, I see him look at me. He asks, "Why aren't you at the doctor's?"

"Like you care," I snap.

"What you did back there was stupid and reckless. If it was a real fight, you'd be dead."

I don't say anything. I'm too tired to argue.

"But that was also brave." His tone softens. "I'm proud of you."

I turn my head and raise my eyebrows, surprised. He lets go of my hand and walks away.

In my room, I go straight to bed. Seems like if I don't lie down, my body will break. I take my communicator and see like a hundred messages in our chat.

'Lorna was a badass today, wasn't she?' A text from Logan. Others seem to agree with him. Everyone thinks it was cool. Probably even Arthur. I smile to myself.

Grace asks if I'm fine.

'I'm alright,' I text. She sends the heart sticker thing. I send a similar one. It's so ridiculous it makes me laugh.

Arthur messages to another chat, *'Tomorrow some of you will go on your first task. I need to check one thing, and I need three of you with me. Volunteers?'*

'Me,' I type. I don't know why, but somehow I'm always the first to volunteer for everything. Logan and Randy volunteer next. Arthur tells us to meet him at the entrance to the main building tomorrow at 8 p.m.

CHAPTER 17

SAFE WITH ME

I woke up at noon today, and after realizing I still had some time, I decided to go for a walk to the lake. Good thing now we're allowed to leave the castle's territory. Not that the restrictions ever stopped me, though.

I follow a familiar path through the woods and get to the lake pretty fast. I see an old deck and go there to sit.

It's so calm here. And silent...

But silence is not what I need right now, so I decide to listen to music. I open the music app on my communicator. It has all the music vampires make. Humans have tons of their own apps, so it's only logical that there should be something for us too.

I scan through the bands and artists. Nothing really catches my attention until I stumble upon a band called *Shadow Warrior*.

I play a few songs and like them instantly. The voice seems familiar, though I can't really understand who it belongs to. I open the info to see who the vocalist is, and it says, *'Lead singer, guitarist, songwriter: Arthur Black.'* I didn't know he was a musician, and damn, he's good at it. That makes me even more into him, his voice is magical. He's what they call *'sings like an angel, screams like the devil'* thing. Yes, I hang out with my bandmates too much. But other people say so too, don't they?

I listen to a couple more songs and like the band even more.

I search for *REBELS* and see my band. We only have 7 songs for now, but people seem to like them. I scroll through the comments and smile. I'm actually doing something that people relate to.

Then I go to the info and see *'Lead singer, songwriter: Lorna Burnell'*. My heart cheers, but something feels wrong. I realize it's my surname. Not mine, actually. A surname of a man who left his own daughter and his wife.

I don't wanna go by it anymore. I correct the info. Now it says *'Lorna Reckless.'*

At 8, I go to the main building's entrance and meet with the guys. Arthur got the intel that the other clan might have a plan to attack us. I don't know why, but there are just two places where they can be. That doesn't make sense to me *at all,* but well... We need to check those places and look for anything that seems suspicious. How do you look for something suspicious when the whole mission seems suspicious?

We go through the woods, past the lake, and I glance at the place where I was sitting just today. We pass the railways and get to the mountains.

We climb up a little, and then we're near the chasm. It's deep, and at the bottom, there's a river. I barely see it, but I can hear it well as the canyon walls create an echo.

"We have to split up now," says Arthur. "Logan and Randy go along the chasm, and Lorna and I will check the cave."

Randy and Logan nod and turn right, walking along the edge. Arthur turns on his heels, not waiting for me.

I start after him, and when I look inside the cave everything inside me twists. I take a breath and move faster to catch up with Arthur. It's already getting dark, and it's even darker in the cave. I take deep breaths, trying to calm myself down.

We turn around the corner, and the dusk sunlight disappears at all. It's dark. Too dark. So dark I can't see anything but silhouettes.

I hold my breath. I feel my heart pound in my chest. And I can't move. I'm so afraid that I feel like my legs are chained. I can't take a single step.

I stare into the darkness and try to breathe. *There's nothing to be afraid of. It's ok. Darkness means no harm. You're not alone here.* I try to reassure myself, but it doesn't really work. But I take a step forward, toward my fear. I can't just stand there afraid. I need to move. Face my fear. I am strong enough to do that.

As I move, my legs are heavy. And I feel like my lungs don't get enough air. I move slowly, like a tiger approaching its prey. But right now I'm not the tiger, I'm the prey. I feel like one.

Arthur is already quite far ahead of me. I stop and lean against a wall. I can't move further. My fear is stronger than me. For now.

Arthur stops and then goes back to me. I let go of the wall and walk towards him. I'm not comfortable with showing my weakness or fear to others, especially not him.

"Are you ok, Rebel?" he asks.

"I'm..." *fine,* I want to say, but I can't. Somehow it gets hard for me to lie now. So I just stare at him, unable to say a word.

"You're afraid of darkness," he says, and I nod, though it didn't sound like a question.

"There's nothing to be afraid of. Come on." He extends his hand. "It's ok. Nothing will happen to you. Moreover, you're not alone."

I hesitate for a moment and take his hand. It's warm even though the air around is cool.

We go deeper, holding hands. My heart pounds, and I don't know if it's the darkness I'm afraid of or Arthur's hand in mine that makes me nervous.

Soon we reach the end of the cave, and I see the weak light coming from above. Moon.

Arthur lets go of my hand, and I turn away from him, looking around.

"Well, it's clear here. Hope Logan and Randy are coming back too," Arthur says, his voice tense.

I look at his face lit with moonlight. His eyes almost glow. I move closer to him but restrain myself in time. Maybe I shouldn't have.

"Let's go back," he says, extending his hand to me again.

As we walk, I already feel calmer with my hand in his. Suddenly, I hear a rustle, and I twitch and squeeze Arthur's hand. I didn't really mean to, but he squeezes mine back. He turns to look at me. "It was probably just a bat," he says, and I lift my head a little to meet his gaze.

"It's okay," he says in a calm, soft voice. I've never heard him talk like that before. "You're safe with me," he says and wraps his arm around me, pulling me to him.

I rest my head on his shoulder, and I do feel safe. For some time, we stand like that. Then he pulls back. "We should go," he says.

When we approach the exit, he lets go of my hand. Logan and Randy are waiting for us.

"It's clear," says Logan, shrugging.

Arthur nods – though I can see he's concerned – and we go back to the castle.

CHAPTER 18

THERE WILL BE WAR

The next morning, we're at the gym as usual. Arthur stands near the window, waiting for all of us to gather, clearly lost in thoughts that aren't pleasant. His expression is grim and hard to read. I wonder what he's thinking about.

"Hey," Grace nudges me with an elbow, and I jump. Too lost in my own thoughts about yesterday. "So, what did you find out yesterday? If anything," she asks.

"Nothing," I say. "Everything was clear." Was it? Maybe I missed something that Arthur's thinking about.

I'd like to talk to him to find out what he knows. And honestly, I do feel like coming to him. Or more precisely, I *would* feel like it if we were alone. So I just don't do anything. Maybe I'll have a chance later.

"Let's begin," Arthur says in the voice of someone who has just been bothered doing something very important. "Today we'll train outside. Follow me." He leaves the gym, and we go after him.

He leads us to where the game with Damian's clan took place. "Now we divide into two teams. One stays here, the other goes with me." Roy, Ruby, Memphis, and I are told to stay.

"Any guesses what we're doing?" asks Ruby.

"No idea," I say, shrugging.

We just stand there, waiting to find out at least something about what we should do. After some time, Arthur comes back to us. "Today you are spies," he announces. "Your task is to get to the tower and press the button unnoticed. Once you're noticed, the game is over."

"Why are we learning how to spy?" asks Memphis, narrowing his grey-blue eyes.

Looks like I'm not the only one suspicious. Arthur's expression darkens at once. Now I see the same man who told us we wouldn't last here on our first day. "Why are you learning to shoot, throw knives, fight? Maybe you don't need to learn anything at all? You can lead the clan instead of me. Come on! Why not?"

At the better times the Arthur, we all know, would say it with a mocking grin, amusing himself by our attempts to ask 'stupid' questions, but now his expression is dark, almost threatening. Memphis opens his mouth again but doesn't dare to say anything.

"No more explanations, experts. Start," Arthur says, and we don't have much of a choice, so we just go towards the tower.

We walk through the woods until I whisper, loud enough for everyone to hear me, "Stop."

When they pay attention to me, I point at Abigail passing back and forth in some distance. We decide to wait awhile, so she goes somewhere, but she doesn't.

"How do we get past her?" asks Ruby.

I try to think of something but I can't. Turns out, I don't know a thing about how to stay unnoticed. My tactic's usually onwards and forwards and damn the consequences, but that won't work here. Shame.

"Well," says Roy, "why don't we just throw a stone or something, so she goes to check? I've seen that in movies."

I like the idea of a distraction, however, "A stone won't be enough. One of us should go and lead her away."

"Fair point. I'll go," volunteers Memphis.

"Don't forget to stay unnoticed," reminds Ruby.

Memphis nods and goes to the right, soon disappearing behind the trees. We all wait in tense silence.

Soon Abigail turns her head towards where Memphis went. She stares into the greenery and then she runs in his direction. It worked.

We quickly go further and soon approach the meadow. We stay hidden in the tree line as I ask, "So, what do we do now?"

"Let's just go," says Roy, and darts off before I manage to stop him. It's the worst idea, even I know that.

"Roy," whisper-shouts Ruby and runs after him, probably to stop him, but of course, it's too late.

"Idiots," I mutter under my breath as I run my hand down my face.

Logan, who was guarding the tower, has already noticed them. Of course he did.

Well... he noticed Roy and Ruby, but not me. I still have a chance, but only if I act fast.

I walk a little back and to the left. I throw another glance at where Logan, Ruby, and Roy are now joined with Memphis and Abigail. She must've caught him, eventually.

They all stand together, chatting, seemingly without a care in the world. I look around to make sure they aren't looking in my direction and that Randy and Grace aren't here.

I run towards the tower as fast and as quietly as possible. Luckily, I don't have to invent any plan of how to get inside. I've already done it once. Same will do.

I approach the tower from the back – where hopefully no one will notice me – and start climbing. I climb to one of the windows – break it again – and get onto the stairs.

I look down and then up and stand there for a few moments to make sure I'm alone.

Then I run up and find the balcony with the button unguarded. Is it just me, or does it look suspicious? Maybe it's a trap.

And then I realize I don't see the button. Where is it? Was it even movable? I saw the green glow today, I'm sure.

I almost panic, though I don't understand why. "Come on, Lorna, think," I tell myself out loud. And the memory of earlier today comes back to me. "The roof," I say. The button wasn't on the balcony, it was the roof.

I get to another wall and start climbing again. This wall is smoother than the one I was familiar with. My feet slip a few times, but I don't stop, anyway.

I'm on top, and here it is. Unguarded. I press the button and hear the bells ring. We made it.

I did.

As I walk out of the tower, I'm met with a wave of applause from my team and Arthur's emotionless face. *Any word?* I think, but somehow don't dare to say. I just stare back at him for a while before Grace distracts me with a friendly, "Hey, you've done it again!"

"Done what?" I ask, as if awoken from a dream.

She makes this like-you-don't-know-yourself-you-idiot face and says, "Won. When no one thought there was a chance of winning."

I smile at her words. Arthur doesn't comment on the situation in any way, and we just return to the castle.

I don't feel like sitting in my room or going out with the guys, so I just go to the balcony – one of my favorite places to think. And I do have a lot to think about.

When I get there, I see Arthur near the railing. He probably likes this place, too. Maybe it's a good opportunity to ask him about his concerns. I come closer.

"Hey."

He turns, his gaze empty and sharp at first, but it softens the second his eyes meet mine. I continue, "What did you notice yesterday that I haven't?" I decide to go straight to the point.

"Why do you think there was something?" he asks back.

I don't feel like saying anything. I know he understands what I'm talking about. We hold each other's gazes for a while before he breaks the contact and turns to face the city in the distance.

"This." He shows me a pendant in the form of an eagle. Does it mean anything? "I've found it yesterday. It's a warning," he says.

"There will be war," he adds and goes silent.

CHAPTER 19

THE WAR HAS BEGUN

The last two weeks went without surprises. The training sessions became harder, though. Arthur definitely prepares us for something, but he doesn't tell us what and when this something will happen.

After that conversation on the balcony, the word *war* rings in my head non-stop. How does he know? It was just a pendant, wasn't it? And what does an eagle mean to him? And who's starting this war? Too many questions, too few answers. I kinda got used to that already. To not knowing anything, just moving forward and doing my best.

Today, we're going to the mountains to learn some survival and mountaineering things, as Arthur said, 'just in case.' We are near the same cave where everything started.

Before entering, I stop, and a shiver runs down my spine. What if Arthur's right about the war?

I hear his voice behind my back. "Any problems?"

"No," I say and go inside.

Inside the cave isn't as dark as it was back then, but I still don't feel very comfortable here. When all of us are inside, Arthur lifts some kind of weapon he was carrying and shoots at the ceiling of the cave. An explosion rings out, and stones start falling down. I cover my head with my hands and duck down to avoid getting hit by one of the rocks.

In a matter of seconds, the cave drowns in complete darkness. "Your task is to get out," rings Arthur's voice in the perfect silence. I can't see the others, but I can feel they are just as stunned as I am.

I hear that someone is trying to move stones, but of course it's no use. We can't physically do this, even with enhanced vampire strength. Conversations start, and the steps are heard.

I hear a rustle from the other side of the cave that startles me and reminds me how scared I actually am, even knowing that all my teammates are here. I suddenly wish Arthur was by my side to hold my hand and calm me down like he did then, when we were here alone.

Everyone is talking and discussing how to get out. Except for me. I think I've heard someone ask, "Where's Lorna?" And I'm right here. Thoughts run through my mind as I stand in the middle of the cave, paralyzed... again. *No, not this time,* I tell myself. *Not again.*

I start moving carefully, cautiously until I reach a wall. Touching its cold and damp surface, I slowly move deeper into the cave, remembering the dead end of it. The dead end with a cavity in the ceiling. This might be a way out.

Soon I get used to the darkness and move more confidently. The fact that I'm doing something to help all of us soothes me even more.

The walk feels endless and when the darkness starts getting less impenetrable, I smile slightly. I'm at the end of the cave, where rays of sun break through the cavity. I let out a sigh.

Do we have a rope? I ask myself, but immediately roll my eyes at my own thoughts. Of course we don't. And it's a shame because it would be very useful. Without a rope, all of us will have to climb. It will take much longer, but I don't see any other option.

I go back to the others, not terrified of that darkness any longer and, without paying attention to their conversations, shout, "I know how to get out."

The voices die down, and Ruby says, "Lead the way." I don't see it, but I hear cheerfulness in her voice. For some reason, it makes me smile.

"I'll sing so you can follow my voice," I announce, and start singing one of my recently written songs.

I head back to the end of the cave, singing non-stop. When we get there, I point up. Without much hesitation, I start climbing. I should've probably said something, but they aren't dumb, they'll get it.

I get to the top uneventfully, climbing already feels as natural as walking to me. The bright afternoon sun blinds me for a few seconds and I look around as my eyes adjust.

Sharp peaks of the mountains are closer than I've ever seen them, occasional spots covered with snow. We aren't high, and looking at those towering shapes makes my eyes widen in childish awe and trepidation. That's the thing about mountains, they look majestic, like they can and will crash you if you don't pay enough respect. If you dare to invade their territory and disturb their peace, you'd better be damn well prepared. Mountains – especially like the ones in front of me – don't forgive mistakes. Why does that make me want to climb to the very top of the world?

Soon we're all out of the cave, waiting for Arthur to come up and tell us his verdict. As soon as he joins us, a bullet whizzes past me. I look in the direction it came from and see about 20 people.

Before I can realize what's going on, they're close to us and their bullets riddle the air. I don't know who they are, but it's clear they were expecting us and they are here to kill. And most of us are unarmed.

When one of them lunges at me, I realize I only have a knife. He pulls out his sword, and I dodge. I pull the knife out of my boot and grab the man by the hand, sinking my knife into it. He drops his sword because of pain.

Without hesitation, I grab it and stand facing the man. He lifts his gun, but before he can pull the trigger, my – his – sword cuts through his neck. He collapses to the ground, trembling, blood floating from his wound. After a few seconds, he stops moving.

I just killed a person. My hands start trembling from the realization as I stare at him, but I don't have much time to calm down or process what I'm feeling. Another three soldiers come at me. One of them lifts a sword, and I hit it with mine. It wobbles uncomfortably in my hand.

Another one comes from behind, and I hit him with my leg, still keeping my arms busy fighting the first soldier when the third one comes.

Like in slow motion, the four of us collide in this dance of death. I try to keep my focus on all of them at once, and by far, I manage. I push one of them aside, dodge another's sword, and simultaneously kick the third one in the jaw. They don't seem to be well trained, considering I can cope with three of them at once.

Two men come at me from different sides. One with a sword, the other preparing to punch. For a second I stand at my place without moving, and when one of them raises his sword, I jump back – right at the approaching woman.

We fall to the ground, the sword I acquired falling from my hand, and she manages to hit my side with her knife, which I haven't noticed before. And then she roughly pushes me off her. I roll to the ground, and for a second, catch a glimpse of one of the men kneeling near the other. Both of their clothes are stained with blood.

Just then, the woman gets on top of me and aims her knife at my throat. I manage to grab her hand mid-air. She's strong – much stronger than I am. I won't be able to hold her hand for too long. Moreover, taking into account that the man rose and is now coming toward us, determination to kill me glowing in his eyes. I dare to let go of her hand with one of mine and hit her stomach as hard as I can. From surprise, she relaxes a bit, and I stab her knife into the ground near my head and push her off me.

Just when the man lifts his sword, I roll to the side, barely avoiding it, and jump to my feet. I run a couple of meters to grab 'my' sword. Before the woman can react, I throw it at her and hit her right in the stomach. For a second we lock eyes, my expression as surprised as hers. Then she falls to the ground, breathless. I hear one of the soldiers command to retreat, and the man with a sword leaves our little battlefield.

When I understand we're safe, I remember about my side. It hurts like hell and is bleeding badly. If I were still human, I would've died from blood loss already. But I'm not just alive, a minute ago, I could fight.

My body screams for me to lie down or at least drop to my knees, but I ignore it and clutching my side look around. Some bodies lie on the ground with blood puddles around them. I scan the crowd to make sure everyone's alive. I sigh in relief when I understand it's actually true, though many are injured. They'll survive, but still.

What the fuck was that?

Arthur turns to go back, and we all follow him. We walk in complete silence, and when we arrive, everyone has this what-the-fuck-has-just-happened look on their faces, but no one dares to actually ask. Neither do I. Not that I'm afraid to or something, just... what's the point?

"I'll tell you everything tomorrow," Arthur says so fast I barely catch the phrase and leaves.

First, the guys go to the hospital for a check-up. I opt out and head to my room instead. I'll heal better without Ms. – whatever her name is – telling me I need a week off.

I decide to lie down, and for a while, I just stare blankly at the ceiling, but soon thoughts start appearing in my mind. The painful realization that I can no longer be the person I was just this morning slowly but confidently downs on me.

I killed two people, there's no way back. There's no way to wash the blood off my hands.

Of course, if I hadn't killed them, they would've killed me without hesitation, but it doesn't change a thing. Self-defense doesn't fully justify anything. There should've been another way. There's always another way. Killing's never the only way out. Just the easiest. Just the one you don't have to invent. It's cowardly most of the time.

Deciding we need some fresh air, we all got to the cliff from where me and my best friends once jumped.

Logan and Randy are doing exactly that. Grace and Memphis are watching the sunset, sitting together on a stone nearby. Ruby, Abigail, and Roy are running after one another. And I'm just sitting at the edge, my legs dangling in the air. I don't understand how everyone is so calm. Or maybe they just look calm, I probably do too. But my mind is racing. I hope Arthur will really tell us something worthy tomorrow.

"Guys," Ruby snaps, "maybe we can all stop pretending everything's fine?" We all stare at her in silence. "Thanks." She sits on the nearest rock, hugging herself, looking pale despite her bright red hair.

No, no one's calm, not even a little. "So, what do you think about all that?" I dare to break the silence.

"I don't really know what to think," says Logan. "It seems Arthur wasn't too surprised about the attack. And if he knows something, why not tell us?"

"He said he would tomorrow, right?" says Grace.

"I believe he should've told us *before* we got attacked," snaps Logan.

I just sit silently, sensing the tension rising. And *'there will be war'* in my head turns into *'the war has begun.'*

CHAPTER 20

I'VE ALREADY TOLD YOU ONCE

The next afternoon Arthur comes to the gym even grimmer than he usually is. And armed.

He scans us, and his look clearly states, *'if someone at least moves, I'll shoot you right here.'*

"We're at war," he announces. "Clan leader Vivian Myers. We once had a conflict in the past." He pauses. "She didn't get enough. Since today, you can't go around unarmed. You can choose your weapons at the armory. Find it on the underground level. The territory restrictions that you had at the beginning are back. Your training is your responsibility now, I won't have time for that anymore. That's all for today." He leaves.

That was... short. I was hoping for a more detailed explanation.

We go to the armory, and my jaw literally drops. Guns, knives, spears, whatever, really. And everything looks just *stunning*.

The armory itself is so big a literal army can fit in here. The walls are made of shiny grey metal and everything seems to glow.

After a few minutes of gawking, I choose a simple black gun, a matching black knife with a silver blade instead of the one I took from my kitchen, and a sword that I simply couldn't walk past. But the thing is that while I feel absolutely comfortable with guns and knives, I'm not really a professional in all those sword things. It was a complete disaster yesterday, I didn't know what to do at all. However, a sword felt so good in my hand. I want to learn to wield it. I *need* to learn.

Night training sessions, hello again.

Days of training with my friends – me, Roy, Grace, and Memphis train together every day, nights of training on my own until one day I hear, "Do you ever stop?"

I turn to face the voice. "Not until I've got everything I want."

"Appreciated." Arthur grins. "And what do you want now, Rebel?"

You, I think and grin to myself but say, "My sword technique is not the best yet."

"Much better than others in your group have, though. I believe a sword is indeed your weapon. You just need more training." Arthur pauses, thinking. "Want me to show you some moves?" he finally says.

I nod. "Yeah." A one-on-one training session with Arthur is something I can't miss for quite a few reasons.

He goes to the gym armory and grabs a sword and then comes back to me. "Well," he says, eyeing me, "first, show me what you've got."

He swings at me. I barely manage to react, blocking his hit with my sword. I hold the hilt with my right hand and support the tip of the blade with my left. Definitely not a smart move, considering my blood is running down to my elbow already, but I have no idea how to block otherwise.

He retreats and swings again, missing my left side just barely – definitely on purpose. He pauses, giving me an opportunity to attack. I swing from the right, aiming for his left side at the waist level. He moves swiftly to his right and takes a step forward, elbowing the back of my neck. I fall to my knees.

"Okay," he says thoughtfully. "That was bad." He chuckles. "Why did you even think all that was a good idea?" He raises his eyebrows in genuine surprise.

"I don't think it was. I just have no idea what to do," I snap.

"Don't sulk about it, Rebel. I wasn't trying to offend you."

"I'm not offended," I say defiantly as I get up and face him.

He rolls his eyes. How much do I want to see these eyes roll from pleasure.

"Anyway," he says, pulling me back to reality. "The first lesson: never do the things you just did."

He explains the basics to me, and that makes me wonder how the fuck I even managed to survive during the fight with Vivian's soldiers. The sword-fighting doesn't seem to be something alien anymore, though. That's definitely a good thing. I love this weapon so much, it feels mine.

After showing me everything a beginner should know, Arthur sits on the floor cross-legged, watching me as I rehearse my moves. It feels uncomfortable at first because he obviously sees and notices every little mistake I make. With time, I stop caring, though, and just do what I have to.

I swing at the air from different directions, practicing different moves and stances. The sword falls from my hand and I jump to the side, trying to avoid it cutting my foot. Then I remember the training sword isn't silver and roll my eyes at how pathetic I must've looked. I pick it up and during the next hour I practice without a care for possible injuries. Just like I should've from the very beginning.

I feel that I'm getting way better. Just a little more practice. A few more hours will do the trick, I suppose. But Arthur doesn't give them to me.

He gets up and says, "I want to show you something interesting now." He smirks, cocking an eyebrow. "This isn't exactly a necessary thing, but it looks cool. What you wanna do is basically slice a throat vertically. Right here." He traces his middle finger from the collar of his T-shirt to his chin. "The trick is to not slice the head in half. You want a rather superficial cut, just enough to draw a lot of blood but not kill."

Such a thing seems rather unnecessary and I'm not sure I will ever use it at all, but I must admit it looks absolutely stunning as I picture it in my head.

He shows me how it's supposed to look. First, the move itself and then he comes to me and slowly traces the tip of his sword up my throat, showing where I need to cut. I hold my breath.

"Try it," he urges as he takes a step back.

I try it for about 15 minutes, perfecting the move on air. I imagine a person in front of me and aim for their throat.

Then Arthur tells me to trace the route on him, so I do. I position the end of my sword just where his collarbones meet in the middle and trace it up. He lulls his head back slightly to grant me access. That's a super casual move, but damn, it looks so good. I want to throw the sword aside and fuck him right here and now. But I'm a trained soldier now, so I restrain myself.

"Now try to actually perform it on me," he says.

"What if I do it wrong and cut you in half?"

He laughs. "It's not even silver. You won't hurt me."

"I'm pretty sure that it *will* hurt if I cut you in half," I tease.

"Good luck with that," he retorts calmly.

I swing, but don't even touch him with my blade. I really *am* afraid to hurt him.

"Come on, Rebel," he says, sounding disappointed.

I swing again, this time drawing a tiny bloody line on him. It heals immediately.

"That was actually good," he says. "Now, let's try it in a fight. That way you can practice other things, too."

I swing at him, and he blocks it for a second before throwing my sword off. I retreat a step and swing again from the other side and he steps away. He tries to hit my back with his sword, but I turn and block.

In a few minutes, I notice that he doesn't even put in any effort. He literally just lets me practice, so unlike him. I make a few attempts at the neck slice move, but he just steps back casually.

Finally, his silent mocking angers me so much that I concentrate on his throat only, measuring the distance with my eyes, aiming. This time I won't fail.

I swing. He bands back slightly, but this time I predicted that. I slice just perfectly, and blood streams down his neck. How much I want to lick it.

"Good job," he praises and smiles, his blue eyes bright.

I smile at my success as well. I'm so ready to become the best swords woman. Adrenaline and excitement pump through my veins. I can't remember the last time I felt so ecstatic.

"Why have you decided to show this to me?" I ask.

"Don't you know?" He smiles at me faintly, as if my question amuses him.

"Should I?"

"I've already told you once."

'You're worth it, Rebel.' Does he really think I'm worthy?

"Listen to me," he says and pauses, waiting for eye contact. When I look at him, he continues, "I don't think you understand what a potential you have. I'll be honest with you, you're the most hardworking person I know. And it has its results. I've already told you, I remember the skill level you had when you came – or more precisely, that you had *no* skills – and now I'm sure I can go to war with you *alone*." He emphasizes the last word.

"You're one of the best already. Not in your team, in general. Believe me, I've met many, and you stand out. Your character, will, bravery, intelligence, and so do your skills now. I've seen you practice just today. More than an hour without a single break. So if you ever think of doubting yourself, don't. I don't think there's anything you can't do if you aim for it. Literally anything."

"Why are you telling me this?" I ask quietly with a doubtful look.

"Because I don't want a person who can actually do something to doubt herself."

I break the eye contact and don't say a word. After a couple of seconds, I ask, "Do *you* ever doubt yourself?"

"Who doesn't?" he says.

"It's not an answer," I demand.

Arthur laughs slightly. "Enough chit-chat, Rebel." I snort and leave.

CHAPTER 21

WAR'S GOT NO RULES

Through sleep, I hear banging on my door and screams. I open my eyes and realize it wasn't a dream. I get up and go to the door.

I open it, and Grace almost flies into my room. Her face is wet with tears, and her eyes are red. She's still crying.

Concerned, I ask, "Grace, what happened?"

She only bursts into tears even more and hands me a piece of paper. I take it and realize it's a letter. It says, *'We have your sister. You wonder who we are? If you're not as dumb as you look, you'll guess eventually. But it will be too late for her, anyway.'* And some numbers below.

By the time I finish reading, Grace has already calmed down a little and stopped crying. "Will you help me?" she asks quietly.

"Yes, of course," I say. "What do you suggest?"

"I already talked to Memphis, he went to Roy to tell him."

Right on cue, we hear a knock on the door, and I go to open it. Roy and Memphis come in.

"So what's our plan?" says Memphis, hugging Grace by the shoulders.

"Do we even know who kidnapped her?" I ask. Grace shakes her head, and then I realize. "Wait," I say. "We know where. The numbers – these are coordinates. Not that I can read them or whatever, but I know someone who can."

I run out of the room, and the others follow me. I get to the main building and down to the basement. I jog into the tattoo parlor.

"Hey, Skylar," I say as I burst in.

"Hi. I see you brought your friends for matching tattoos," she says, looking at the guys.

"Oh, I wish our visit was so pleasant," I say, and her face darkens. She's surely worried. I continue, "You once told me that your girlfriend is good at computers and all that shit, right?"

"Yeah," she says thoughtfully.

"Can she help us?" I ask.

"I think..."

She calls her girlfriend, and I show her the numbers. We decided not to tell the whole story. It's better to not talk about it too much, just in case.

Soon Evangeline says, "Well, I've found something, but..." she trails off. She's worried, maybe even frightened. "What is this all about?" she asks, her face concerned and serious.

"What you found?" I ask, ignoring her question and staring at the screen. She understands that I won't tell her anything, so she points at the monitor and says, "You were right, these are coordinates. Of an abandoned warehouse." She exhales heavily. "It belongs to Vivian Myers' clan." Same clan that recently attacked us. It can't be good, but not unexpected.

"How to get to that place?" I ask, determined.

She explains the way with a heavy look, I thank her, and we leave.

We're in Grace's room. She sits on the bed with Memphis, and Roy sits on the floor. I stare out of the window. All of us deep in thought.

"We can't just go there. It's suicidal," I say finally, like a sentence. "We need help."

"But whose?" Grace asks. "We're all here already. Who else can we ask?"

"Is there anyone else you trust?" asks Memphis. "I mean, from the team."

"Not really." She pauses. "Not with that at least," she corrects herself immediately.

"If it's Vivian, then the kidnappers are powerful. Too powerful for us. I think we should tell Arthur," I say and bite my lip.

"What?!" Grace jumps from the bed. "Are you crazy?" Everyone looks at me in bewilderment. "Why do you even think he will help? He never will."

"We should try," I say. "We don't stand a chance without him. It's just logic."

"Absolutely not," says Grace in a stern voice. I've never heard her speak so coldly. "We'll go tomorrow and save my sister. Only we four. Lorna, are you in?"

That's madness, I think. "Of course," I say.

We stay for a little longer to think of strategy, but we don't have any experience, so it all comes out lame. We go, we see what's out there, we act. I mean, I'm not a stranger to inventing a plan on the run, but I'm not stupid either. Now's just not the fucking time for that. A kid's life is at stake, it's too much of a risk.

"We should get some rest before tomorrow," I suggest, and everyone agrees.

I sit on my bed, thinking. Tomorrow. Tomorrow we'll sign our death sentence. I'm sorry, Grace, but I can't just wait and then kill ourselves on this mission. My instinct tells me I'm making the right – or at least the best – choice.

I go to Arthur's room. I don't know why, but I'm sure he will help. Maybe I trust him too much, but I can't think of any other option.

At the door, I hesitate, but then I remember that Luna's life is at stake and open the door without even knocking. When I enter, I see Arthur standing near the window. He turns around and looks at me. He's calm as usual, but I see he's surprised.

"So now you break into my room in the middle of the night without knocking?" he asks.

"I need your help," I state, trying to ignore the fact that he's standing in front of me shirtless in the semidarkness. Now's *really* not the time.

"Help? With what?" Well, at least he's not shutting me out right away.

I bite my lip before I say, "Grace's sister was kidnapped."

"Why is this my problem?" he asks, but I can see that it's just about showing off.

"She was kidnapped by Myers' clan." I say that to make even his arrogance interested in helping me, though I know he'll help, anyway.

He's silent for some time, and then he says, "Tell me."

I tell him the whole story, though I don't know many details myself.

When I finish, I look at him, waiting for his answer. But instead, he just stares back at me.

"I'll help," he says finally.

I sigh with relief. He goes to one of his other rooms. In a minute or two, he emerges with two guns. Really good ones. I've never even held anything like that in my hands. And here I thought the armory had the cool stuff.

"Take it," he says and hands me the weapon. I take it from his hand and my fingers brush his just slightly. His body, covered with black ink tattoos, is so close to mine and for a moment, the world disappears.

But I break my trance and ask, "Do you have a plan?"

"Just go and kidnap her back. I don't think they want to kill her. At least not right now. So we've got a pretty good chance. They want to give us a scare." He takes a breath. "They want us to know they have access to our families. Want us to know that the war is coming and they have their own rules to play by."

I just nod in acknowledgment.

We didn't say a word on our way here, and now Arthur's loading his gun and saying, "There are two entrances. I'll go left, you go right."

"How should we get her when she's found?" Suddenly, I feel so helpless and worthless. I don't know how to do anything. If I can't even help a friend, how can I help anyone at all? I bite my lip to keep from crying.

"Hey," Arthur says in a low voice, almost a whisper, "I have no doubt you will cope with it. Just do what you always do." He looks me in the eyes for one more second and then heads toward the building.

He can see my doubts, can see I'm nervous. I try so hard to hide it, that it probably stands out even more to him. Seems like he knows a thing or two about hiding emotions. And if he understands what I feel, why does he reassure me? It's true after all, I don't know how to do things the right way. I always mess up. Like with the fence, like during our fight. The only thing I actually did was manage to press the damn button, but even then I blacked out after.

'Just do what you always do.'

I doubt myself too much, I have to stop this.

In the company of my thoughts, I find the door. I take a deep breath and open it, keeping my gun ready. It's dark inside, and the air feels damp. I look around cautiously and listen to every rustle. I'm not sure if it's my nervousness about the darkness that makes me overcautious or the desire to find Luna to prove my worth to myself.

I hear a weak moan behind one of the doors and go in the direction of the sound. At the door, I stop, paralyzed by my doubts about my abilities. Even though I'm feeling weak now, I suddenly wish Arthur was here to help me. But he's not.

So I try to open the door on my own. It's locked, so I decide to break it. I kick with my foot and the wood splinters.

In the room, I see a redhead girl. It's probably her. I approach and notice that her arm is bleeding badly.

"Hey, Luna," I whisper. The girl seems to be surprised that I know her name.

"Who are you?" she whispers weakly.

"I'm your sister's friend," I say. "I'm here to he-" I don't have a chance to finish the sentence. Someone hits me from behind, and I black out.

I hear a female voice. I try to move, but my legs and arms are tied. I open my eyes and notice we're in a different room now.

I see a man and a woman – who look like bodyguards – armed with guns. And another woman with them. She is tall and has blond hair. Her face is pierced literally everywhere.

A thought pops up in my head. *Luna! Where's she?*

Ignoring the woman and the guards, I get up a little and look around. Luna's also here, unconscious. Of course, my reckless act didn't go unnoticed. It was stupid to let my guard down.

"What's your name?" the woman asks, her voice is low and raspy.

I turn my attention to her. "Who are you?" I ask, ignoring her question.

She grins a little and comes closer to me. She hits my face with her boot, and I fall to the floor, wincing. She takes a gun out of her gun sling and aims at Luna. My heart pounds in my chest. Realization hits me. Vivian.

"What will the death of a human child bring you?" I ask, getting up again. No answer, but she hesitates.

"You are her," she says knowingly. "The girl Carl can't stop rattling about. You made him kill his brother." She must be referring to the battle near the cave.

She grabs me by the throat and almost lifts me. It's not the first time someone is choking me, but her grip is tighter than Arthur's.

By the way, where *is* he? Is he alive? Of course he is. He's a good warrior, after all.

"Why don't I just kill you as a payback for their lives?" she says. I stare confidently at her. Her eyes are deep brown, full of anger and desire for revenge. Then I hear a moan. Luna's awake.

Vivian lets go of me and smiles. "I wanna play." She gives the man a sign, and he cuts the ropes on my legs and arms.

"Get up," she says, but I don't need an invitation. I lunge at her, grab a knife from her waist and aim at her, but of course, her guards hold me down. One of them hits my stomach and face.

"Don't hit too hard," says Vivian. "I need her alive. For now." She grabs the collar of my T-shirt, making me stand up from my knees. She gives me the knife and, nodding toward Luna, says, "Kill her."

I can't hold back a laugh. "You really think I would do that? Why would I?"

"We'll see," she answers. She stabs my arm and nods to the guards.

They both beat me until I'm bleeding and bruised. From time to time, Vivian asks if I'm ready to kill Luna, so they will let me go. Of course, she doesn't get the answer she wants. Soon I understand there's no reason to fight back, I can't win this. But maybe I can buy some time for Luna so Arthur can save her.

Damn, where *is* he?

After some more beating, I'm beginning to lose consciousness. I fight so hard to stay awake because I know if I black out, Luna will not have a chance of survival.

Half-conscious, I hear a bang, and the door flies open. Without hesitation, Vivian leaves through the back door with the woman. Arthur enters the room, his eyebrow bleeding and his lip split. Before the man reacts, Arthur shoots at his head.

I try to get up, but my legs fail me, so I almost crawl to now awake Luna to free her from her restrains. "It's over," I say. "You're safe."

She nods weakly, "Thank you."

Arthur approaches us and squats. "How are you?" he asks.

I wanna snap at him because the question is indeed stupid right now. But I restrain myself. It's easy to see he's actually worried.

"Alive," I answer and smile, unexpectedly even for myself.

"Can you walk?" he asks, and I nod. Like I have a choice. He helps me get up, takes Luna in his arms, and we leave.

In the early morning, we're back at the castle. "I'll take Luna to Grace," I say.

Arthur nods. "Get some rest after," he says.

I go to Grace's room and knock on the door. She opens.

"What's that, Lorna?" Her face becomes concerned. "What happened to you?" she asks, probably noticing my bruised hands and face.

"Nothing. Just someone wants to see you," I interrupt her and wave to Luna to come closer.

"Luna!" Grace exclaims, and hugs her sister. "How did you do that?" she says.

"Doesn't matter," I reply. *Just did what I always do.*

I feel like she wants to ask something else, but instead she says, "Thank you."

I just nod and smile. I leave them alone.

I realize I didn't even thank Arthur for helping me. I want to go to his room, but first I need a shower and to change my clothes. And after I've done that, I feel so exhausted that I decide to lie for a second and fall asleep.

CHAPTER 22

LET THE SCARS REMIND YOU

When I wake up, it's already dark. I slept through the whole day and missed my training session with the guys. I still need to talk to Arthur, though, so I get dressed and go to his room.

I knock on the door and hear his voice. "Who's that?"

"It's Lorna," I say.

"Come in."

I open the door. Immediately, I say, "Thank you for your help. I wouldn't have done it without you."

He nods and approaches me. Our eyes lock.

"Why did you ask me to help you?" he asks.

"I..." I pause. "I understood that we didn't stand a chance against Vivian. As a leader, you know how to handle her in the right way. I didn't want to mess this up."

"Well, you did all the job though, didn't you?" he says.

"What? She would've killed me *and Luna* if you hadn't come in time."

"Wasn't that the plan?" He laughs at me.

Nice. Like I don't know myself that I did bad.

He rolls his eyes at seeing my expression. "I'm tired of reminding you all the time what a good warrior you are. I wouldn't have had a chance to save Luna if you hadn't taken the fall for her and bought me time. Do you really not realize that?"

I bite my lip fast. I don't want him to notice, though I know he does. I don't know what to say, so I just stare at him.

For some time, he looks back at me and then presses his lips to mine. One of his hands wraps around my waist and the other settles on my neck. At first, my instinct is to pull away, but I don't want to. So I kiss him back, awkwardly wrapping my arms around him.

When he breaks the kiss, he presses his forehead to mine, his eyes closed. I close mine too. We stay like that until he steps back a little to look at me. We lock eyes again, saying nothing.

I gather all my courage, put my hand on his cheek, and finally dare to say, "I love you."

I know it's weird. I know it's too fast. I know I should probably say that I *like* him, not *love* him. Although, call me crazy, but I feel something way deeper than *'like'* for him. I guess I just haven't fully admitted it to myself yet. But now that I've said it to him, there's no way back. I'll take all his sarcasm and remarks. He kissed me first, so he should deal with the consequences.

But to my surprise, he replies, "And I love you."

My eyes round for a second, and he brushes my nose with his. "Thanks for saying it first, I would never dare," he admits.

You're welcome, I guess. I'm too startled to form any reply right now. I'm pretty sure it's written clearly on my face.

He kisses me again, so gently. This time, his hand slips under my t-shirt. And apparently I don't mind it there. His other hand travels to my thigh and then down my leg. He lifts it to his hip, and I wrap it around his waist as he lifts me. He kisses my neck and whispers in my ear, "I want you."

A breath hitches in my throat. I've been dreaming of this for weeks, then why am I so nervous?

"Take," I whisper shakily.

"We don't have to do this if you're not ready, or don't want to, or whatever else. You know that, right?" He looks warmly at me.

Obviously, I understand that, but him saying it makes me melt. But I do want it and I won't let this stupid nervousness get in the way.

"I want it," I say quietly, chewing on my bottom lip. "I want you," I say, confidently and louder this time. I know how to show confidence while shaking inside.

He smiles at me, and we kiss again as he carries me to the bedroom. It isn't very spacious and is dark: black furniture, walls, and even bed sheets. Panoramic windows line one wall, black curtains on both sides. The full moon peeks into the room, illuminating it silver.

Arthur lies me on the bed and hovers over me and then kisses my neck. His lips are warm, and I feel every part of me that they touch burn with an electric tingle. It feels divine.

I slip my arms under his sweatshirt and pull it off him. I put my hand on his chest to stop him for a while. I wanna look at him, take it all in, and savor every second.

His body is perfect, flawless, damn. His neck, arms, and chest are covered with black ink tattoos. Despite the tattoos, I notice scars. Some are small, some bigger. I hope I will know their stories someday.

I take my hand away, and he pulls my T-shirt off me and then my bra. He covers my upper body with kisses as I reach for his belt. My hands shake slightly, but I manage to unbuckle it and undo his zipper.

He leans back and kneels on the bed between my legs. He pulls my pants and underwear down my legs and I instinctively press them together. He throws my clothes on the floor.

He undresses himself and gets back on top of me, his body pressed to mine. My still trembling hands roam his upper body, and I bury my fingers in his hair. He kisses my neck and runs his hand down from the side of my ribcage to my thigh. He's so gentle with me that I don't even recognize him.

"Is everything alright?" he asks, checking on me.

Don't get me wrong, it's sweet of him but also kind of annoying. "I'll tell you if something's wrong, okay? Don't bother, I'm not a little girl."

He smirks. "That's my Rebel. Spread your legs for me."

I do as he asks, though I hate the fact that I'm giving him what he wants so easily. I think I'll have to correct this little mistake in the future.

He slides inside me slowly, gently, centimeter by centimeter. I can't hold back a gasp and clutch his shoulders. I don't think I even want to hold back.

Arthur moves gently, caressing my body with his hands. In some time, all adequate thoughts leave my head, and all I can do is moan into his ear. Something tells me he doesn't mind.

He feels better than anyone ever did. And I realize that he's finally mine. All mine.

"I love you," I whisper in his ear and pull him closer. Fuck, I love him so much. I want to dissolve in him. It feels awesome to let it out.

Some time later, we lie in bed next to each other, trying to get our breathing back to normal.

"Come here," he says, stretching his arm to me. I move to lie on his chest, putting my hand on it, and he wraps me in his arms.

It's the first time in my life that I feel this way. Like I've finally found someone with whom I belong. The thought that it's too early to feel this way doesn't leave my subconscious, but I push it even deeper because what I'm doing feels right.

"I love you, my Rebel," Arthur says.

I raise on my elbow and look him in the eyes, and then kiss him. "I love you too," I say as I pull away. I lie back on his chest.

After a while, I ask, "Why me? I mean, I thought you hated me."

"And I thought you hated me," he says with a chuckle.

"I maybe used to, but somehow I felt that there was something more in you. Right now you're not the person I thought I knew," I say.

"Right now I'm real," he replies in a low voice. "I want you to know who I am. Who I *really* am. I..." He pauses. "Even though I've never really done this, I'm ready to let you in. If you want me to."

"I do," I say, rising on my elbow once more. "And I'm also ready to let you in. Somehow I trust you. I don't know why, I know it's stupid. I've never trusted anyone like that."

"Same. And I don't think I've ever really loved like that. Not in a long time anyway," he says, smiling sadly.

"How's that? How old are you even? I mean, you look like you're 25 or something, but I'm sure you're older."

"I'm 217."

"Wow," I say.

"What? Am I too old for you?" He laughs.

"No, of course not." I laugh too. "Just how come you've never loved during such a long life?"

"I mean, I have. Obviously. Just not the same way. How should I explain it?" he says, laughing.

I've never seen him laugh sincerely. Almost never seen him even smile for real. Not when it's just a cold mechanical grin. "I've never seen you laugh," I say.

"I don't have many reasons to laugh," he says, and his smile disappears, and it was so beautiful I already miss it. Instead, now when I look him in the eyes, I see the depths of his soul, the centuries of pain he carries with him. I want him to share his pain with me, but for now, I don't dare to ask.

After a pause, he says, "You can't imagine how much I'm broken. What I've been through. All the pain, loss... Not that I actually had a reason to live. I'm not even talking about smiling."

"Tell me your story," I decide to ask after all.

He closes his eyes and bites his lip. "Okay," he says and takes a deep breath.

"My mother died when I was 7. It was long ago, but I still remember her well. She was a wonderful woman. Kind, loving, caring, smart, strong, very brave." He smiles. "I remember how she looked at me and said that I have my father's eyes, but mine are more blue. I remember how she laughed." His eyes become wet, his gaze distant.

"When I was 7 and my older sister, Aurora was 18, my mom was killed. Shot while she was walking. At that time, I didn't really understand what happened. The only thing I learned fast was that

I would never see her again. When I was older, my father told me that she was killed by the clan we had a war with. My father was a good man, too. He was like a best friend to me. For a long time, he was the only one I could talk to.

"When I was 15, I lost my sister. She jumped into the chasm on my mom's birthday. Poetic, right? We didn't have a perfect relationship, but it still hit me hard.

"Some time later, I fell for a girl. It was my first love, and it *really* got into my head. We were dating for a while and then she betrayed me. It was a knife in the back." He shakes his head and laughs. "Literally. She hugged me and stabbed me with a knife."

I raise my eyebrows, refusing to believe it.

"Turned out that she was with the enemy clan," he explains, "and they told her to kill me. That was the last drop for me. That was when I stopped trusting anyone. People betray too easily. I swore to myself that I would never ever fall in love again, never let anyone in. And I managed. Before I met you." He fixes his eyes on mine and holds me a little tighter. "There was something in you I didn't want to resist. Something that made me feel like I can risk trusting you. Like you will understand." He touches my cheek.

"I love you, Lorna. You're doing something to me I cannot explain. You make me feel alive. You make me *want* to live. All my life I've been waiting for the day I die. I was ready to. And now, for the first time, I feel like it can get better. You're giving me hope." Tears well up in his eyes, and I barely hold back myself.

Here he is – always so cold and composed – telling me about all his downs, all his pain just because I asked.

"I love you," I say. "I will never let you down." I kiss him.

For a while, we're both silent, and then he continues, "My father, he died not so long ago. About 70 years. He burned in his own house. The same clan that once shot my mother took my father, too. They took *everything* from me." As he says it, tears run down his cheeks. I've never seen him cry before. I didn't even think he could cry. He looks so vulnerable now. He *is*. I lie beside him and hold him close. He lays his head on my chest, and I wrap my arms around him. I feel my body get wet with his tears.

"Hey," I say gently, "thank you for telling me. You're not alone now. Not anymore."

"Thank you," he says and rises on his elbow beside me. He kisses me, and he tastes salty because of the tears that are still falling from his eyes. I put my hand on his cheek and wipe his tears away. He covers my hand with his. Then he takes a breath and wipes his face with a hand. All emotions disappear from his face in a second.

"So, what's your story, Lorna?" he asks.

I look at him uneasily. I never told it to anyone. But I trust him, and I want him to know. "Well, my story's not as long as yours, but I do have one, unfortunately." I say, staring at the ceiling. "When I was 4, my dad left us. Mom said that he died, but I know it's not true. I heard them arguing the day before. I saw him leave. I don't know why she said he was dead. Probably she didn't want me to feel abandoned." I sigh.

"I never had a good relationship with my mother. She never loved me. Never cared about what I wanted. Always said I had to get married and have kids while I was dreaming of becoming a warrior." I look at Arthur, and he smiles slightly.

I point to the scar on my right thigh. "See this? That was when I said I wanted to join the army. She hit me with a spoon she was using for cooking. It was hot, and a blow was pretty hard, so I got a burn and a bruise. It wasn't the only time." I can't hold back the tears and start crying. It's hard to think of those things and even harder to say them. Arthur wraps his arm protectively around me.

"See these scratch marks around it? I hate this part of my body so much that I always scratch it with my nails. Over and over. I've wanted to get rid of this scar because every fucking time I saw it, it reminded me of the fact that I don't have a family. That my own mother hates me."

I put my hand on my leg and dig my nails into the skin, crying. Arthur covers my hand with his, stopping me from hurting myself. He takes my hand away, then leans down to kiss my scar. He looks up at me. "Let it remind you of how strong and beautiful you are."

"Thank you," I whisper. "You finally make me feel loved. Make me feel like I finally have a chance for a family. With you, I feel home. I love you, Art."

"Is that my new nickname?" he asks, smiling.

"If you don't mind."

"I definitely don't." He kisses me, and I don't want to let him go, so I wrap my arms around him tightly. Soon I drift off in his arms, warm and safe.

CHAPTER 23

MY BLOOD AND BONES

I wake up in Arthur's bed but alone. It's still dark outside, the light's only begun to creep up the horizon.

I hear the faint sound of an acoustic guitar and Arthur's voice barely louder than a whisper. I get up and wear his T-shirt that hangs on a chair. I inhale, and it smells like him. Would it be too much to only wear his clothes from now on? I smile at my thoughts.

I go carefully – as if to not scare the music – to the living room and see Arthur on the balcony. Quietly, I come closer. I don't want to interrupt him. His singing voice is enchanting. So I just stand there listening and catch some lines:

"You're a lighthouse in the ocean

A reminder that I gotta fight

You're the one who can accept my demons

The only one to ever see my tears

I'm not sure that I have earned forgiveness

But I am braver with you next to me"

When he pauses to write something down, I say, "Good morning."

He turns his head and smiles at me. "Good morning, Rebel. Have you been standing there for a long time?"

"A while," I say, smiling.

He lays down his guitar, gets up from the floor and comes to me. He puts his hands on my waist and kisses me. I bury my hand in his hair.

When we pull apart, I glance down and see the *rebel* tattoo with a small heart next to it. I look back up at him, a silent question in my eyes.

"Just wanted it to remind me of you even though we weren't together then," he says, as if reading my mind.

So it *is* about me?! I can't believe what I'm hearing. One must be crazy to get a tattoo reference to someone they aren't with. Crazy like me, I guess.

I kiss him again. "I have something like that, too." I show him my tattoo. "I got it to admit to myself that I loved you. But truth be told, I don't think I actually ever admitted it until I told you."

He takes my hand in his, smiling. We kiss once more and then stand for a while with our foreheads pressed together.

Then I rest my head on his chest. The sunrise is amazingly beautiful now. The sun is red – illuminating us in a scarlet glow – and the clouds are painted orange and yellow, the sky is green and blue.

"What do you think about a lemonade?" Arthur asks suddenly.

"Can't say no to that," I reply.

He leads me to the kitchen, and I sit at the table as he makes us lemonades. Vampires don't have to eat in a human sense, but we still can do that if we feel like it. And we obviously still need water to survive.

Arthur puts a glass of lemonade in front of me, and I take a sip. Oh my god, this is heavenly. Please, don't tell me this man is also good at cooking, I don't think my heart can survive that. Is he actually bad at anything? Oh sure, feelings.

But then I remember all the things he told me last night. I feel like I know his deeper, most private parts, but at the same time don't know him at all. What I know for sure, though, is he trusts me. And it's good because I trust him too.

I just sit in silence, staring at the table in front of me, lost in thoughts, until Arthur's voice pulls me back to reality. "Are you alright?"

"Yeah." I pause. "Yeah, I was just thinking."

"About what?"

"About last night," I say, lifting my eyes to his.

"And what were you thinking, exactly?" He takes my hand.

"Nothing in particular, just taking it all in."

He only smiles as a response.

"Your smile is so beautiful," I say.

"Not as beautiful as yours."

And just like that, I'm smiling too.

I ask, "Hey, will we tell anyone about us?"

"Do you want to?" he asks back.

I just shake my head almost invisibly. I don't really know the answer myself. On the one hand, I don't want to tell anyone, but on the other hand, there's no logical explanation for that. I just don't want my friends to stick their noses into my life and ask tons of questions. But if so, are they really my friends? I mean, I don't trust them enough to even tell about my boyfriend.

My thoughts are interrupted by, "I don't want to tell anyone either."

I sign with relief. Partly because I didn't have to decide this.

"Want me to show you something?" he asks.

"What's the something?" I return.

"Yes or no?" Arthur says, smiling mischievously.

"Okay. Yes," I say, furrowing a brow. I don't want to put this debate any further, even though it amuses me.

"Then meet me at the entrance at 7."

At 7 p.m. I'm at the entrance, waiting for Arthur. When he comes, I say, "You're late," and grin. He rolls his eyes at me.

"Shall we?" he says and offers his hand to me. I take it, and he leads me to his car. A shiny black sports car... I really need to ask him to let me drive it.

The ride goes uneventfully and soon we arrive... somewhere. Nothing seems special about this place. Arthur gets out of the car.

"So?" I say, questioningly.

"Ready for a warm-up?" he asks with a wave of his hand and starts running. Quickly, I get out of the car and follow him.

First, we run through the forest, then go up a hill of a mountain. From time to time, I have to jump over tree roots and climb rocks. Don't know what Arthur is up to, but I definitely like it already.

I get out of the woods right on his heels and find myself at the top of a mountain. My jaw literally drops as I take in the breathtaking view in front of me. Below us lies the city, above us the endless sky, and on the horizon, barely discernible from the sky, is the sea.

Seeing my expression, Arthur offers me a smile. "Do you like it?"

"Joking? It's *amazing*." I hope we're lucky and the sunset is beautiful today.

We wait for the sun to set, talking about everything in the world, occasionally stopping to kiss. The sunset really happens to be a wonderful one. Orange sun, pink and purple clouds.

"I never thought of you as someone who likes such things as a sunset," I say, and Arthur laughs.

"Seems you imagined me to be not the person I am at all."

And I still managed to fall in love. "Yeah," I sigh. "Why are you hiding yourself?"

He bites his lip. "I don't know. It's easier that way. It's... less painful. I don't know."

I sit closer to him and hug him by the shoulders, resting my other hand on his knee. "Why do you trust me with this, then?"

"I just feel like I can, that's it. Like you'll understand." He sighs. "Or maybe I'm just so tired of hiding that I want to *believe* you'll understand," he adds, voice sad.

You and me both... I hope so much we will work out.

I kiss him deeply. "I love you," I say.

We don't talk much until the sun sets fully, going for cuddling and kissing instead of conversations.

When it's already dark, Arthur gets up and offers me his hand. Instead of taking it, I wrap my arms around him, and he returns the hug. I bury my nose in his neck and inhale his scent. A trace of perfume and shampoo, he still smells just like I remembered.

After a couple of minutes, we start walking towards the forest, and I grab his hand to calm myself. When we enter the territory of shadows, Arthur lets go of my hand, but only to hold me by the waist, closer to him.

"Don't mind if I drive?" I ask when we see his car.

"Go ahead," he says and throws me the keys. I smile at him as I get into the car. I start the engine, and we take off.

I press my right foot harder and harder with every second until we drive at about 200 kilometers an hour. The road is empty, so I let myself gain a little more speed. It's been a long time since I drove last. I smile to myself as I remember learning to drive. How awkward every move was and how insecure I probably looked. Though I understood at once that cars are my type of thing.

I decide I don't wanna go back yet, so I turn in the direction of the sea.

"Where to?" Arthur asks when he realizes.

"Surprise," I answer, and he chuckles.

I drive to the place where cliffs stand right by the sea. One of the most beautiful places I've been to. Every time I'm there, I think of meeting the sunrise. I feel like it will be amazing. But I still haven't done it yet.

I park not so far from the ledge and kill the engine. Turning my head right, I see Arthur looking at the distance. "Beautiful place," he comments, and I smile slightly. He gets out of the car and walks to the edge, and I follow.

For a while, we just stand side by side, watching the dark waves and the starry sky above. In such places, I feel like the world belongs to me. I feel my strength, power, freedom. But usually those come with a pinch of pain. It's slight but never leaving, drilling. The pain of being left alone, being unable to share my worries, being maybe even unlovable. But *now*, now I have someone to share this world with, someone to call my home. Someone who understands, supports, empowers.

Someone who is not just unafraid of the strong woman I am, but who respects me exactly for that. Someone as broken as me, with so many stories that will never be told, with so many regrets, losses, mistakes, so many scars, and still with a heart of gold. Someone who, just like me, is afraid to look in the mirror, waiting for the day the dark side will take control. Someone who might save me and I might save him.

I take Arthur's hand and look at him. "I'm so grateful to whatever it is that I have you," I say, and he returns a slight smile.

It's pretty cold outside, so soon we go back to the car, and I sit in the passenger's seat.

"Going home?" Arthur asks.

"Yeah." I nod.

Though after about 15 minutes of drive, I say, "Pull over."

He does, and with concern evident on his face, asks, "Why? Is everything alright?"

I nod and take his hand, lifting my eyes to meet his. I reach across the car to put my other hand on his neck and kiss him. He returns it immediately as his hand travels to my waist. I lower mine to his ribcage and pull him toward me by his T-shirt. He breaks the kiss, but only to get himself to my side of the car, and I move my seat back to make space for him.

Arthur gets on his knees and looks up at me. "What do you want me to do? Tell me. I'll do anything."

I smile at this suggestion. "Weeell, first, I think this," I pull at my T-shirt, "is really unnecessary."

"Got you," he says and puts his hand under my T-shirt to pull it up and take it off me. Same fate awaits all the other items on me.

"So?" he asks.

"So," I echo.

I put my hand on his head and guide him between my legs. He kisses the inner side of my thigh, and I feel his breath on my skin. I sigh.

He kisses me a couple more times, and I lower my hand to his chin to lift his head. I slide my thumb over his lower lip, and he licks my finger.

Suddenly, I think that so many people would assume our roles should be reversed – women submit, men dominate, and all that shit – but why would anyone care if we're both satisfied? And I feel like asking, "How do you feel?"

"Good," he whispers with a small smile. "Too good," he adds, closing his eyes.

I'm not sure I could say the same in his position. I'm so not a submissive type that I can hardly even imagine that. But well, if he's good, I more than don't mind that, so I lower his head back and pull him closer to me.

"You know what to do," I say, and he indeed *does know*.

He eats me like he's been starving for months, and my pussy is the only thing that's offered to him.

He grabs my thighs and digs his nails into my skin. The barely noticeable and yet such sweet pain makes me press his head even closer to me. He bites lightly on my clit, and a moan escapes my lips.

I can't stand the distance between our bodies anymore, so I say, "Come to me. I want all of you."

Like a trained soldier he is, he follows my command immediately. I press my lips to his and dig my nails – that I almost don't have – into his back. I pull his T-shirt off him and unzip his pants sliding them down his legs just enough.

He enters me, and I moan into his mouth. He moves slowly, gently, and it's starting to get annoying. "Stop being so gentle," I command.

He looks at me for a second, grins and lifts my hands above my head, increasing the speed and intensity of his moves. That's better. I bite his lip because of how good he feels.

"If you want my hands to remain there, you will have to hold them," I say through my moans.

He smiles wickedly at my words and goes even harder.

"Art," I breathe into his ear, writhing beneath his hold. "You feel so fucking good," I praise. "Don't ever stop. I want more of you. I want *all* of you."

"Good thing I wasn't planning on stopping then," he replies, his voice shaky against my lips.

He kisses me and starts exploring the inside of my mouth with his tongue. I take his lip between my teeth and bite hard enough for his blood to leak onto my tongue.

"You're driving me crazy," he says. "I want to fucking devour you."

And unexpectedly, even for myself, I realize I don't mind if he does. In all possible senses.

My orgasm builds and I lift my hips to meet his, chasing the pleasure. He grabs both of my hands in one of his as his other hand lowers to my clit.

"Oh fuck," I mutter when he touches me and in just a few seconds, he sends me over the edge, following right after.

He lets go of my hands and pulls out of me, and I don't think I've ever felt so empty.

He asks me to move so he can sit, and I position myself on his lap – bending my legs – and put my head on his chest, curling up like a kitten. He wraps his arms around me and kisses the top of my head. "I love you," he whispers into my hair.

I smile and ask, "You want more, don't you?"

"What do you mean?"

"When we have sex," I clarify. "You want more."

He's silent, so I continue, "It feels like you're holding back, like you're hungry for something more, something else."

He sighs. "All this lovemaking, it's new to me. I love things rough, I love when it hurts. I love to take it to the limit. I have a gentle side to me, as you've seen, but there's also the side of me that demands that I..." He trails off. "That I break you," he finishes in a whisper.

"You know, I want that," I say, lifting my eyes to his. "I'm not a very gentle person either. Don't get me wrong, it's good to have that *sometimes,* but I don't mind if you hurt me. I *want* you to hurt me," I admit. "Don't *ever* hold back with me."

"Are you sure about this?" Arthur asks.

"I'm sure," I say confidently. "Break me."

CHAPTER 24

BROTHER

At the gym, Grace comes to me and hugs me. "Lorna, thank you again for saving Luna. I can never pay you back for that enough."

"Oh Grace, um… you know I had to. You've thanked me once, I appreciate it. No need to do it constantly. It makes me feel awkward." I laugh. "Moreover, it's not completely my merit," I stutter out.

She frowns at me. I bite my lip. "Arthur helped me," I admit.

'What the hell?' is written on her face. A thousand silent questions hang in the air. I just shrug and smile awkwardly.

"Well," she says finally, "maybe it wasn't such a bad idea after all."

Roy and Memphis come to us, and I'm extremely happy to see them now. At least we don't have to continue this conversation.

We decide to make a small competition today. Keeping things fun and all that. So we invent an obstacle course that includes running, shooting, and climbing.

"I'll go first," I say enthusiastically. I'm so competitive I even annoy myself sometimes.

Grace sets the timer and yells, "Three! Two! One! Go!"

I start running. One circle around the gym. Two. Three.

Then I run to the shooting section – almost tripping on a sword someone left on the floor. Arthur would be furious if he found out someone just drops their weapons wherever they please.

I grab a rifle and load it. I fire, hitting the first target perfectly. I take a few steps back – to make more distance between me and the target – and fire again. I do the same thing three more times, then unload the rifle and put it back on the counter.

I take off to the climbing wall. I get into the harness and start my climb. I love doing this a lot, so I'm excited as I go up. At the top, I push myself off the wall and jump – safely flying toward the ground.

As soon as my feet hit the floor, I take the harness off and start climbing again. My speed doesn't falter even without safety. It's actually thrilling to experience danger like that. Makes me feel alive.

I get to the top and then climb back. I giggle to myself as I think that I could've very likely forgotten there was no harness on me and just jumped. What a ridiculous way to die.

I run to where the guys stand. "So, how long was it?"

"5 minutes," says Grace.

"Cool," I say. But I can do better.

The guys do the same course. Grace finishes in 7 minutes, Roy in 5:30, and Memphis in something close to 8.

When the guys leave, I stay for a little longer. I have more than two hours before meeting with Roy for a walk, so why not train a little?

I repeat the course like ten more times, shortening my time to 3:45. I decide that I need some rest and go to idly throw knives. When did something like that become relaxing?

"Hey soldier," Arthur calls to me from behind, and I turn to face him.

"Hey," I say.

He looks around as if making sure that we're alone, closes the distance between us in a few long strides, and kisses me. He turns me slightly, pushes me a little, and I take a couple of steps back.

He presses me against the wall as his hand slides under my T-shirt. He steps even closer to me and presses me flush against his body. I'm losing my mind.

He deepens the kiss, and it becomes more demanding, his tongue slips in to explore my mouth as if he hasn't done this a thousand times already.

He traces with his lips down to my neck. I smile and dig my nails into his back.

He nibbles lightly at my neck and asks, "Can I?"

"Can you what?" I ask.

He licks his lips, and I realize what he wants. I nod.

He kisses my neck again and then sinks his fangs into my skin, holding my neck steady with his hand, just like he did during the turning. Tingle spreads through my body as he drinks me. It feels so good.

He licks the bite wound and I feel the blood drip down my neck. Vampire saliva prevents wounds from healing, so this won't heal fast.

He kisses me again, and I taste my own blood on his lips. It awakens hunger in me like I've never felt before. I break the kiss and look at him.

Then I lick his lip and bite his neck without asking for permission. Sorry, not sorry. He's mine now, I'll do whatever the fuck I want.

I take a gulp and another and one more. His blood tastes better than anything else I've ever tasted before. It's not the first time I'm drinking blood as a vampire, it's been weeks since I've been turned. But this... This is something different. It feels so intimate and he tastes so familiar.

I lick his neck and break away, trying to catch my breath. I rest my head against the wall. "You feel too good," I say through my panting.

He puts his hands on the wall on both sides of me and kisses me. I feel like I'm trapped here, between this wall and his body. And I fucking love that.

"So, you train through all of your free time or what?" Arthur asks.

"Almost." I giggle.

"Yeah," he says, "of course not all the time. You still need it to do some shit with your friends, right?" He smiles sarcastically.

"Right," I snap. And duck under his arm and start walking away.

He grabs my hand to stop me, turns me to him and settles his other hand on my waist, looking at me questioningly.

"What?" I say.

"You understand I was joking, right?" he says.

"Were you?"

"Lorna, I'm just worried about you, okay? I won't try to stop you from having fun with your friends, I'm just asking you to be careful."

I nod. He kisses my forehead and lets me go. It should be settled, but it feels like it's just started. And that scares me.

"Grace told me that Arthur helped you with Luna. Is that so?" Roy asks, and I nod. "Why were you so sure about his help?"

"I just thought I'd give it a try. That's it," I say.

We're silent for a moment, both of us staring at the dark woods beyond the castle fence as we sit on the steps leading to the main building.

"It surprised me he actually helped," Roy says.

"It didn't surprise *me*," I say matter-of-factly.

"Really?"

"Uh-huh." I pause. "He can be an asshole. Most of the time," I decide to add, and Roy laughs. "But he's better than this. Do you not notice?" He shrugs as a response. "He would do this for any of us. He can behave like an arrogant jerk, but he's a man of honor," I say.

Roy looks at me, puzzled. "Since when do you think that highly of him?"

Since when? I ask myself. Since he told me he respected me? Since Damian told me Arthur saved him? Since he let me join the army? Since I saw respect in his eyes when we first fought?

"I knew it almost from the beginning," I say suddenly, the revelation surprising even for me. "Just never really paid attention."

Roy just mumbles, "Maybe."

"You know what else Grace told me?" he asks mischievously.

"What?" I ask. Do these two just gossip all the time?

"She said that you might like him."

I look at him as if what he just said is complete nonsense.

"Relax." He nudges me. "I know she just imagines that."

I bite my lip. "We're dating," I say. I risk looking at Roy to see his more than stunned face.

"You what?!" he asks.

I shrug. "What's so non-understandable?"

"How you and Arthur can end up together," he says, louder because of his shock.

"Well, I came to his room to say thanks for helping with Luna and-"

"Wait, wait, wait," Roy interrupts me. "What was the reason for coming to him? Couldn't you like... thank him wherever else?"

"I forgot. And then drifted off. That's why I missed the training."

"So, you came to thank and..." he trails off.

"And we talked for a while, and then he just kissed me. I returned the kiss because I didn't mind." I smile.

"Damn." Roy laughs. "I can't believe it."

"Ah, by the way, don't tell anyone, okay?" I say quickly.

"Not even Grace and Memphis?" he asks.

"Not even them," I confirm.

"Okay. I won't," he answers. "So how is it to be with someone who's the hottest guy in town?" Roy laughs.

I laugh too. "Good," I say. "It's nice to think that while everyone wants him, you're the only one who actually gets," I joke.

"By 'want' you mean..." he trails off, a sly smile on his face.

"Actually, I meant like 'wants to be with him.' But your version also applies." I smile.

"Wait, so you have..."

"Damn, stop talking like it's a forbidden topic," I say. "Yes, we have, so what?"

"It's just way too strange to think that way about you and Arthur. Moreover, it's been just 2 days."

"Too fast for you?" I laugh.

He smiles, rolling his brown eyes. "And how is he?" Roy asks.

My eyes almost roll into my head from pleasant memories. "Best," I say. "You know, he's not the person we think he is. He was so careful and gentle with me." *Before he wasn't,* I think, but leave that to myself. "Who could guess?" I smile slightly. "He's an amazing person. All I've ever wanted," I say.

"Damn, I could imagine you talk that way about *anyone* but Arthur." I shrug. "Anyway," he says, "I'm happy if you are."

"Thank you." I hug him.

It's nice to share what's on your mind with someone. I think Roy's my best friend, after all. A brother in some way.

By the time we've returned to the residential building, we've hit a couple of jokes, and now we can't stop laughing. We go up the stairs, chatting and laughing so loudly I think we've already woken everyone. I laugh so hard I have to stop and lean on a wall when I hear footsteps.

"Ooo, someone came out to kill us," I joke, and we laugh even harder.

"Hey, you two, don't you know it's the middle of the night?" Arthur's voice rings and echoes in the building.

"My joke about being killed doesn't sound so funny anymore," I say through laughter. I literally *can't* stop. I look at Roy and see the same going on with him. He tries so hard to restrain himself, but fails.

"Hey," Arthur barks as he reaches us. He grabs my hand. "What's even going on? You'll wake everyone up."

"Sorry." I laugh and put my hands around his neck, literally hanging from him.

"Excuse me?" he says, stunned, and doesn't even hug me back. He's good at holding a disguise. I let him go and look at Roy. We just start laughing harder.

"Enough," says Arthur, irritated. "To your rooms, now. Roy, you live on the second floor, do you not?"

"Do you know where everyone lives?" I ask, surprised.

"Only those I need to keep a close eye on," Arthur snaps.

"We were going to Lorna's room, actually," Roy says.

"Really?" Arthur asks, amused. I nod. "I think you'd better not. You both are waking up early tomorrow," he says, now grinning.

"What do you mean?" I ask hesitantly.

"You're on the patrol tomorrow morning."

"What?!" me and Roy say together. Arthur just smiles. I roll my eyes. And finally, stop laughing.

"Arthur, really? For what?" I say.

"For the sake of protecting territory."

"You know what I mean."

"Have no idea," he replies, his eyes bright with amusement.

"Whatever. Roy, shall we?" I say and hug Roy by the shoulders. We turn to go up the stairs.

"Will you ever stop challenging me?" Arthur asks.

I turn my head. "No," I say, smiling, and he smiles back at me. For a while, we just stare at each other.

"Maybe I should leave you?" says Roy.

"Wait," I say, and come to Arthur. I put my hands on his shoulders. "Hey, I know you're angry, but we didn't do anything bad. Maybe we can not patrol tomorrow?" I say playfully, my voice sweet.

"You're acting weird today," he says, frowning.

"I know." I laugh. "You know you'll have to get used to it," I add, still smiling.

"Okay," I say, turning to Roy, "I'll see you tomorrow." He smiles and nods. "Good night." I wink at him.

When he disappears from sight, Arthur pushes me away from him. "What the hell was that?" he asks.

"I'm just in a good mood. You should try it someday," I snap. Nothing's left of my good mood now, thank you.

I look at him. "You're such a downer, Arthur."

"I just thought flirting in front of your friend was not the best idea," he explains.

"He knows," I say.

He sighs, annoyed. "Couldn't you tell me, huh?"

"I just wanted to have fun," I say a little louder and leave to my room.

"Lorna, wait!" Arthur says, but I don't listen. "Lorna!"

I go faster up the stairs. Today we argued two times. For how long can we go on like this? I feel tears prick my eyes and blink them back. When I reach the door to my room, Arthur catches up with me and makes me stop.

"What's wrong?" he asks. I turn away. He slides his hand on my cheek before turning my head to face him. He raises his eyebrows at me as if reminding me I didn't answer. On impulse, I wrap my arms around him, and a couple of tears fall from my eyes as I press myself into his body.

"Well," I take a breath, "first, I don't want to hide our relationship. I just realized that I want to be free when I'm with you. You know, I want to hold your hand in front of my friends or kiss you in public." I pause.

"Okay," he says.

"Okay?" I ask, surprised, as I lift my head to look at him.

"Yes. No problem," he repeats.

I stare at him. "I didn't think you'd be fine with that."

"Well, I am. I don't care, really," he says, brushing my tears away, smiling slightly. "What's the second thing?"

"We argued two times today," I say and fall silent.

He sighs and bites his lip. "I don't know what to do here," he admits. "Both of us are short-tempered and too proud to admit to being wrong and stop arguing. I'll try my best, though," he says.

"I don't know if *I* can," I say and want to break away, but he stops me.

"Just promise you'll tell me what worries you if there is something," he says gently.

"I promise," I say, and we kiss. "I love you," I say.

"And I you," he answers.

In the morning, I meet Roy outside the castle to go on patrol. We have to cover quite a territory. The time passes quickly though, since we spend it chatting and laughing.

We might be at war, but I haven't seen any signs of it since the weird attack at the cave and the pointless kidnapping of Luna. Or maybe I've just convinced myself all is fine.

CHAPTER 25

24TH OF FEBRUARY

Me, Roy, Grace, and Memphis have met in Grace's room for a friends' night. I love those and they get especially fun when we play truth or dare.

Memphis' turn to pick. "Truth," he says as we all sit at Grace's kitchen table.

Roy is the one to ask. "Well, well," he says, scratching his chin in theatrical thinking motion. "What is the one thing you hate the most about each of us?"

Wow. That's a cool question. I actually want to hear the answer.

Memphis visibly stiffens. He's so sweet. I'm pretty sure admitting something like that is difficult for him.

"I hate the most about you that you behave like a child. Far not always in a good way," Memphis says to Roy a little too irritably. I'm sure he hates Roy for asking that question more than for anything else.

Roy just snorts as a response.

"As for Lorna, I'd say it's the same. But while Roy is simply an idiot, you make every situation worse by arguing, even if you know you're wrong."

I really want to keep my face neutral, but I feel my eyes round in surprise on their own. I want to say something, but I have no idea what, so I just settle for "Okay."

"And Grace," he pauses, "I hate that you're so amazing that I can never be worthy of you."

"Aw, you're so sweet," she says and hugs him. Is she really buying it? I wouldn't.

"Okay, Lorna, what will it be?" asks Memphis.

"Dare," I say confidently.

"Go to our group chat with Arthur and text that you're in love with Randy. Make it look like you were going to text Roy and accidentally sent it to the wrong chat."

I laugh. "You got it."

I open our chat and type, *'Don't be stupid, Roy. You know what it feels like to be in love with someone. I literally can't concentrate when Randy's around. He's just so fine. I want him to be my boyfriend so bad.'* I show Memphis the text, and he nods in approval. I click 'send.'

"To be honest, I'm curious what Randy's reaction will be," I say.

"Imagine he's in love with you," says Grace. "Maybe you can start dating after this. He isn't bad."

Oh, I don't think Arthur will like this idea. Actually, I'm curious about his reaction as well.

My communicator vibrates in my hand from the text from Randy. So tactful of him to make things private.

"Hey, you must've accidentally sent the text to the wrong chat. I really hate to say it, but we will not work out. I'm truly sorry. But to make things sound a little better, it's not about you. I'm just… gay," I read the message to the guys, and my eyes widen in surprise. "Wow," I say. "I wasn't expecting *that*. What should I answer?"

"I think you should tell him the truth. I feel kind of bad that we just made a guy come out like that." Grace laughs.

"Yeah, I'll tell him." I start typing and my communicator buzzes again. And so do my friends' communicators. It's the group chat, it's from Arthur.

'Excuse me? Can someone tell me what I'm seeing here?'

The four of us read the text, and Memphis asks, "Is there something wrong with people from the team dating? Why is he mad?"

Oh, I know why. I just shrug.

'Lorna, I can see that you have read my message. I'm expecting an answer.'

"What do I say?" I ask the guys.

"I have no idea," Memphis says, confused. "What explanation does he even want?"

Another text from Arthur: *'Fine, don't answer. But let me remind you that you're mine and I'm not good at sharing.'*

My eyes round in surprise for what feels like a hundredth time this evening as they stay glued to the screen. Did he just tell the entire group chat that I belong to him?

I quickly text, *'Everyone, all is fine, it was just a dare,'* and send. I lift my eyes slowly from the screen and meet my friends' stunned gazes.

"What the fuck?" mutters Memphis.

"My thoughts exactly," Grace agrees.

"Uh, we're dating?" I say, as if I'm not sure.

I didn't think their faces could get more surprised, but apparently it was possible.

"You're *dating*?" Grace echoes. "For how long?"

"A few days," I say.

A few silent seconds go by like hours. That's exactly why I wanted to keep it a secret.

"So I was right!" Grace exclaims excitedly. "You *were* into him."

I laugh slightly. "Yeah, you were," I admit. "I think I'll go try to sleep. I am on patrol duty tomorrow. *Again*," I say. The guys nod.

Let them gossip about my relationship without me. I leave the kitchen and go to my makeshift bed in Grace's bedroom. I could go to my room, but we like staying at each other's rooms after such gatherings.

I decide to listen to music to help me fall asleep. I turn my communicator on and see a private text from Arthur: *'A dare, huh? You should be careful with those, Rebel. You might just as well end up bent over my knee for that.'*

Is he joking? Damn, I hope not. I just stare at the screen until he asks, *'What happened to the talking-back brat I love so much? Cat got your tongue?'*

I haven't yet seen this side of Arthur, and fuck, I love it so much. But I have no idea what to answer. He's doing things to me.

'Worried I'd like Randy more than I like you?' I text, knowing it doesn't make any sense.

Arthur sends a few laughing faces. I can hear his dark laugh and amused low voice in my head as I read his next text: *'You have no idea what to say, do you?'*

Should I admit he's right?

'It's fine, you don't have to admit it now. I'll fuck that admission out of you when we meet,' he texts.

'I'll hold you to that,' I text back, smiling to myself. He makes me crazy, damn.

For the next half hour, I toss and turn, trying to fall asleep to no avail. Guys run around the room and shout so loudly it's louder than the music in my ears. Assholes.

When they finally lie down, I start drifting off. I have to wake up in 3 hours. Fucking perfect.

I lie with my eyes closed, still listening to music. I feel movements. They're fooling around *again*. I roll my eyes in my mind. They have zero conscience.

A hand touches my leg, shaking it. I turn and bark, "Oh, now what?!"

Grace motions for me to turn my music off. "Listen," she says and goes silent, pointing at the window. "Bombings," she adds in a whisper, half concerned, half nervously excited.

At first, I don't understand a thing. I hear some bangs in the distance, like the low drum. Then the realization dawns on me.

Cannon.

I get up and join the guys at the window. We stare out into the darkness, listening to the blows. One, two, three...

We look at each other. I see fear in the eyes of my friends. I feel only a little nervous. Maybe it's not that bad. I hope it's not.

We look carefully, trying to see some evidence of what we hear, but there's nothing. Just the occasional low rumble.

I sit down on the couch, thinking. "So this is it?" I say. The guys just shrug.

"Messages in our chat," Memphis says. Everyone else has woken up too.

All of us share concerns as the chat goes wild with discussion. I just read silently. Chill runs through my body. Now my own fear emerges somewhere deep inside. I *am* scared. My heart beats a strange rhythm in my chest. I'm nervous, but I try to hide it.

We sit in the room together, throwing phrases about what's going on from time to time. Nervousness rises and I want to cry. Literally cry my soul out, but I don't let a single tear fall. I want to scream, but I maintain coldness and calm as I speak. I try to make jokes, probably just to make myself feel better, but they go out crooked. My own laugh stranded, a little too hysterical.

In some time, I really start freaking out. I talk too loud and too commanding. Grace now took my joke-cracking. She does it better, to be honest.

"Why no one tells us anything? It's been like an hour," I say. Grace shrugs.

"Maybe Arthur's sleeping," says Memphis.

"How can anyone still sleep after those sounds?" I protest.

"I think it's not the first time he hears war. I think he's used to it," he suggests.

"How can anyone get used to something so terrible?" My question goes unanswered.

I look at the guys and notice Roy's eyes are wet with unshed tears. I've never seen him cry before. I never thought he's capable of it even. My first impulse is to reach out to calm him down, but then I think it's better if I don't. He probably doesn't want to show his tears.

Our communicators ring at the same time. I take mine, and a video pops up before I even manage to do anything. All of our communicators have a system that allows Arthur to transmit emergency messages if need be.

In the video, he says, "I'm sure I didn't wake you up. There are those who've done it before. The clan of Vivian Myers bombed our territory. We're officially at war. Everyone should be ready." The screen turns off.

"So this is it?" I say, my voice breaking.

Roy comes to me and hugs me. Then Grace and Memphis join us. We hug like it's the last time. I refuse to believe it.

"Ah, stop it, we'll be just fine in a couple of days. Weeks at most," I say, but hug them anyway. I see tears in Roy's eyes and sweat on Memphis' forehead.

I barely hold back my own tears now. I don't want to hold them back. But I do it anyway because the idea of always being strong sits too deep inside me.

I say I wanna go to my room but go outside instead. It could've been an amazing morning. The sunrise is beautiful. They lie when they say in books and movies that nature mirrors the mood. On the contrary. It is so peaceful now. It lays still as all we know is falling apart.

Tears well up in my eyes. I try to blink them back, but this time I fail.

My mom always said that at such moments we should pray. Pray to the god above that it gets better. It was never an option for me, but now... Now, if this guy exists, I truly hate him. Why pray to someone who allows all of this to happen? If he exists, he's an asshole. If he exists, he doesn't care.

I take one more breath of the morning air and go to my room. I take a shower and drink blood to have strength, just in case. I still don't want to believe it's happening, but I know I need to be prepared. I get dressed in combat boots, jeans, and a T-shirt. I take a knife and a gun with me.

I lie down and cover myself with a blanket, my gun lying next to me on the pillow. Suddenly, I feel too cold. Probably nerves. I hear shooting in the distance, and the sound scares me. In some time I drift off, though the sleep isn't deep.

When I wake up, it's already evening. I decide to go to Arthur's apartment. He opens the door and encases me in his arms at once, and I return his embrace. A tear rolls down my cheek.

He kisses my temple and says, "We'll get through this."

I nod. "I'm scared," I admit.

"I know," he says softly, holding me closer. I stay with him for the night to not go insane.

This day – the 24th of February – I will remember forever.

CHAPTER 26

ROOKIE

Five days went peacefully. I mean, if you can call time at war peaceful at all. Cannons and shootings are always heard in the distance. Arthur said our clan is already directly engaged with Vivian's, though it's not that bad yet.

With time, I even stopped paying attention to the sounds. Like I got used to it. It kinda scares me. How do you get used to something like that? I don't want it anymore. *I want it to be just a bad dream. I want it to stop,* I scream in my head. The ocean of emotions boils inside me, unable to get out.

I sit on the bed, texting Grace. She seems to be getting used to it as well. Then I hear a loud blow and jump on my bed. And just like that, I understand that I'm still afraid. Fear just became different, but it's not stronger.

I run to the window to look. I don't know what I expect to see there, but I do it pretty often. There's this kind of unhealthy curiosity and excitement about that all. Like I want to see the war myself. Though, at the same time, more than anything, I want all of this to end.

In two days, I'm going to the battlefield. I'm both curious and afraid. But I'll have to do it, anyway. So now I'm devoting all of my time to training. I need to be prepared as best I can be.

I wake up from a not-so-deep sleep. I get dressed, take my things, throw a glance in the mirror, and leave.

I walk outside and to the main entrance, where I see the military track that's supposed to take me to the battlefield. I swallow at the sight of it. I crack my knuckles nervously and approach.

A man I've never met helps me get inside. I say a quiet, awkward "Hi" to those already there and take a seat between two soldiers. The realization of what I'm doing downs on me more and more with each second. And my fear intensifies just as fast. It's one thing to listen to explosions while being safe inside a castle fortress and training for theoretical fights, but actually going into battle is a whole different story.

The track door slams shut after a few more people get inside, and we start moving. I take deep breaths in an attempt to calm myself. I close my eyes and think of the last few days. When I wasn't training, I spent most of the time in Arthur's room – unfortunately quite often without him since he is obviously overly busy now – apparently even simply being there calms me down. It's a shame he couldn't see me off today, but he took his time with me yesterday, saying how proud he is of me and how sure he is that I will do well.

The closer we get to the frontline, the louder the sounds become. The ground shakes slightly – or not so slightly – from occasional blows.

The door opens, and the man from earlier barks, "Lorna, your stop."

I get out of the track. We've arrived at the campsite. Just several tents for sleeping. I look around, thinking, *What am I even supposed to do now?*

"Hey you," a girl says from behind me. Bold head, almond-shaped eyes, snow-white skin.

"Hey, I'm Lorna," I say.

She smiles. "I know. I'll just call you a rookie."

"Is it that easy to see?" I ask, a little embarrassed.

She nods. "It's fucking written across your forehead." She pauses. "But it's fine. I'm Annika. I'll show you your sleeping place."

She leads me to one of the tents, and we get inside. There's nothing but 4 bunk beds and a set of drawers. Kind of reminds me of our room as trainees, just even less luxurious.

"It's just me and you here for now, so choose whatever bed you like," she says. "Except for mine, obviously."

I smile. "Thank you."

"Have to go. Later." She takes a shotgun and leaves the tent. I sigh with relief for some reason.

When I'm settled, I go to meet the commander of my division. I find him near the... whatever the machine that launches rockets is called. Damn, I'm bad at terms. I'm bad at names as well, but I've managed to remember that the commander's name is Harley.

When he notices me, he smiles, his light brown eyes lit with undisguised excitement. "You're Lorna, right?"

"Yes," I say, "I am."

He comes to me and shakes my hand. "Welcome to the division. I hope you have fun." He giggles and hits my shoulder in a friendly manner. I feel like I might actually like it here.

"So what am I gonna do?" I ask.

"Your task will be to operate an air defense complex." He gestures at the machine behind him.

Wow. "Cool" is all I manage.

"We'll start your training tomorrow," Harley says.

"Why not today?" I ask.

"Well, if you're so excited, I can't see why not," he answers and smiles even broader. "Okay, let's get inside," he says.

We sit on the bench near the control panel with different levers, buttons and screens. My mind starts to spin immediately. How on earth am I going to understand and remember all that?

First, Harley shows me the screen that'll show me the targets to hit. Then he explains what a few different buttons and levers are responsible for. When the basics are covered, he tells me to try – without actually launching anything, obviously. I get so invested in the process that I lose track of time completely.

"You're getting better at that. I'm actually surprised," Harley says, smiling.

"Thanks, I guess?" He kind of said I was good, but at the same time admitted he thought I wouldn't be. Honestly, I don't blame him, I didn't think I'd be good either. Happy to say I was wrong.

"You will start your work tomorrow," he says.

I nod eagerly, my worries from earlier almost nonexistent in his company. Such a ball of sunshine this guy.

After the lesson, I return to my tent. Annika is also there. "So, how was your first day?" she asks.

"Cool. I've learned how to operate an air defense complex."

"On the first day?" she asks, surprised.

"Yeah... why?" I ask, just as surprised.

"No, nothing." She pauses. "It's just not so common to actually learn things on your first day. Usually, newbies take their time and delay the learning as much as possible. Are you so eager to get involved in battles?" She laughs a little.

"I don't want to stand by when I can do something," I say.

"I see..." she says quietly, her expression thoughtful.

I get ready for the night and go to bed. For some reason, I feel excited about tomorrow. So I fall asleep imagining what might happen.

CHAPTER 27

LAUNCHER

I wake up at 6 a.m., get dressed, and go to meet Harley. He gives me my tasks for today and shows me the complex I will be operating. *My* complex.

I get inside the machine and once again take in all of the levers, buttons, and god knows what else. My training didn't cover all of it. Harley said that for the beginning, I don't need it. I want to know, though. All of it. So I was extremely happy when he added that we'd keep training.

I switch on the monitors that show the sky. Thermal, scanner, map. So many things. As Harley explained, when a target gets into my area – I have a very specific sector I'm responsible for – I will see it on my screen as well as get the warning from soldiers in other sectors, if they notice first, so I can shoot the target down. My monitors show more than just my sector, but I'm to stay within my area under any circumstances.

The first 15 or so minutes go uneventfully, and after I get bored with staring at the screens, I start humming some melodies to while away the time. Obviously, I'm still looking at the monitors, though.

Suddenly, the radio comes to life and a female voice says, "2 rockets coming to sector 5." Then silence and I tense, staring at the monitor and listening.

Then another voice, "1 coming to sector 2."

Then another, male this time, "2 coming to sector 7." Mine. I startle as I hurry to answer "Copy" and focus on destroying my targets.

In just a few seconds, the first rocket crosses the border of my sector. I take aim and launch. In seconds that feel like hours, my scanners show that the target was hit.

I just shot down my first target. Although I don't get time for joy as I aim for the second one. And miss. "Fuck," I curse out loud.

I aim again and hit it this time. "Sector 7, targets destroyed," I say and smile to myself. I think I'm enjoying it.

For the next few hours, I just sit there, shooting down occasional rockets. I didn't realize there were so many.

"10 rockets coming to sector 2," a panicked but at the same time collected male voice says.

"14, sector 5," another one follows.

A few other voices join to announce more rockets, some of which change course. 4 come to my sector. I shoot them down fast enough and look at the monitors.

Sector 8, which borders mine, is overflowed with rockets. Only on the part visible to me I see 10. There's no way they can shoot them all down. So I decide to break the order of minding my own business and aim for the rocket in 8. I hope it's not too far for me to hit.

I launch and hit the target right before it flies into some village.

"Everyone stay in their sectors," an angry voice growls, but I ignore it as I aim for another rocket, hitting it after a second attempt.

I see another rocket in my sector and focus on it first. When it's down, I get my attention back to sector 8 and destroy yet another target that isn't mine. I know I'm getting in trouble for that. But I did what I thought was right. They wouldn't be able to shoot everything down on their own.

It's the end of my shift when I get out of the complex. I'm met by Harley.

"Wanna explain yourself?" he asks. He doesn't have to tell me what it is about, I already know.

"I did what I thought was right," I say calmly.

"That was against the orders. That was chaos."

"They wouldn't have shot them down. All those rockets would've exploded. Did my actions harm anyone?" I ask confidently, but inside I'm begging for him to say no.

He smirks. "No." I let out a relieved breath. "The opposite, actually. You saved quite a few people today."

I raise my eyebrows at that. "You know, I'm not supposed to praise you for disregarding orders, but between us," he pauses, "you did well. I'll make sure to mention it to Arthur," he says, leaving me with the widest smile plastered across my face.

A question pops up in my mind. I run to catch up with Harley.

"Hey, I've got a question," I say.

He nods. "Sure."

"Why do we mostly use swords or guns when clans have so many weapons you can use from afar and with more effectiveness and so on?"

"After the Great War, leaders agreed that heavy weapons should not be used and conflicts should be decided between armies, not civilians. That's it, basically. Just that easy." He smiles.

Well, that makes sense, to be as careful as possible in the situation that's the opposite of careful, but "I don't see that from Vivian. She uses whatever she wants, from what I know."

"Yep," Harley says grimly. "You can't really force everyone to follow the rules, right? Especially if we're talking about war. Wars got no rules if you think of it."

I nod. I really want to see the world with no wars. And now that I have immortality at my disposal, I hope I will. I hope I can help make it possible.

CHAPTER 28

HOMECOMING

My air defense duty goes on for two months until it's time for me to take a break and go home for a week. I'm really happy about it. My job stopped being fun after a few weeks. After hours and hours of thinking, I've decided that when I come back from my time off, I won't stay behind. Time here did me good, I'm not afraid anymore – or at least I convinced myself I won't be. I want to fight on the frontline.

I sleep for almost the whole ride to the castle. I'm exhausted.

When I open my eyes, a familiar sight of the gothic building comes into view. I get out of the truck, almost stumbling over my own feet.

I go to my room through half sleep. "Home sweet home," I mumble. I take a quick shower before I plop on the bed and drift off.

I go in and out of sleep a couple of times before I wake up completely. I feel pretty well-rested, however, the what-year-is-this feeling doesn't leave me for a while. I hate it.

I force myself to tidy my room after noticing the monthly amount of dust on my table. And then I nestle on the floor with my guitar – I missed her so much – and write a few new songs. The closer you get to the epicenter of war, the more you see, so I have quite a few things to say.

Someone knocks on my door. I put my guitar on the floor and get up. When I open the door, I see Arthur's smiling face.

"You weren't even going to visit?" he teases right as I throw my arms around his neck and hug him tightly. He hugs me back.

"Come in," I say and pull away from him.

"So, how was it?" he asks, sitting on the edge of my bed.

"It was awesome," I say, excitement filling my voice.

Arthur smiles at me, surprise on his face. "Harley told me you did exceptionally well," he says.

"It's good to hear." I should probably talk to him about wanting to go to the frontline.

"Do you want to keep this position for now or try something new?" he asks, as if reading my thoughts.

"Actually," I say slowly, "I was thinking of the frontline." I pause. "I'm ready," I add quickly.

Arthur nods thoughtfully. "Not that I wasn't expecting that," he says. "I love your enthusiasm and the desire to fight, but I also worry about you. I hope you can understand that." He pauses. "Anyway, let's talk about this later, okay? Come here," he says, making a gesture with his hand. "I haven't seen you for two months after all." He smiles.

"Missed me?" I tease as I sit on his lap.

He kisses me gently. "Terribly," he says.

I bury my hand in his hair as we kiss. His tongue slips into my mouth, exploring. He growls quietly before pulling away. He looks into my eyes, and I realize how much I actually missed him.

"Can you stay for a while?" I ask, and he nods.

I take off his shirt and run my hands over his chest. He tries to lie back and hits his head on the wall. "Fuck," he curses, and I laugh.

"Are you sure you're a trained warrior? You seem to get beaten by that wall way too easily," I joke.

He makes this careful-what-you-say-to-me face, and I bite my lip. He puts his hands on my hips, lifts me, and throws me onto the bed next to him.

He leans into my ear and whispers, "How was it to live a whole two months without an opportunity to challenge me?"

I giggle. I try to quickly invent some smart-ass remark, but all my words seem to slip away when he talks to me like that.

"Um... boring?" I suggest.

He laughs darkly and slides his hand into my sweatpants. I gasp when his fingers brush the skin just above my panties before sliding inside. Arthur slowly pushes his finger inside me. I close my eyes from the pleasure of feeling him.

He takes his hand out of my clothes and, looking me straight in the eyes, licks his middle finger clean. I almost orgasm at that view alone, and he smiles at my reaction.

"Take off your clothes," he orders gently. I decide to just do as he asks.

Apparently, I am more than fine with letting him lead in bed. I was surprised when I found that out. But the level of trust we have makes it comfortable for me to let everything go.

I get up from the bed and take off my T-shirt and then my pants. Arthur never takes his eyes off me.

"Like the view?" I ask, not even slightly uncomfortable with his staring.

"Absolutely," he says.

"Your turn," I say. And he undresses himself in front of me. At first, I hold his gaze, but then I just go roaming over his gorgeous body with my eyes.

I step closer to him, and he envelops me in his arms, kissing me. He lays me on the bed and goes on to covering my body with kisses, occasionally telling me how amazing I feel.

"I want to roam every inch of you with my mouth," he says.

"Go on then," I urge.

He goes from my neck down to my toes – stopping only on my pussy to give a thorough lick that leaves me only needing him more – not missing almost any spot.

Then he goes back up so our bodies are pressed together and enters me. I lift my hips to meet him. I missed how he feels so damn much.

I touch everywhere I can reach and hold him as close as I can with my already shaking legs as he fucks me. He kisses my neck and my collarbones.

We interlace fingers, and he pins my hands to the sides of my head. For some reason, it always makes the sensations more intense. His name slips from my lips, and he moans in response.

I could never imagine simply saying someone's name can feel this heavenly, but his name feels exactly that way.

"Art," I breathe into his ear one more time.

"I fucking love how my name sounds when you sigh it into my ear," he says through ragged breaths. He lets go of my hands, and I encircle them around him once again.

I got even more exhausted than I was before. But at least this exhaustion feels absolutely amazing. Arthur said he'd stay till morning, so I happily drift off, safe in his arms.

CHAPTER 29

JUST IN CASE

Since everyone from our team came from their posts too, me, Grace, Abigail, and Ruby decided to meet, just the 4 of us. Just the girls.

"So, ladies," I say, "tell me about your tasks, positions, posts... I wanna know *everything*." I'm genuinely interested to know all that. Not just because they are my friends, but because I want to know as much as I can about all those military things. Just in case.

"What we do isn't exactly exciting, but it's not too difficult either, and we can gossip while doing it," Abigail says. "By the way, there's this one guy at our unit."

"Abigail!" Ruby interrupts her.

"Oh, come on, do tell," Grace chimes in.

"See? They're interested," Abigail says pointedly to Ruby, and the latter rolls her eyes. "He's unbelievably hot. Dark hair, blue eyes, tattoos. I melt every time I see him."

"Wait, did you just describe Arthur?" I ask, barely holding back a laugh.

"What? I have a type," she answers defiantly.

"Anyway, what we do is prepare weapons: loading, cleaning, repairing, and all that. I didn't realize how much work it actually is. But I like it," Ruby says.

"Yeah," agrees Abigail, "I do too. We plan to keep our post for as long as possible."

"Me and Memphis have been operating drones," says Grace after a moment of silence. "Honestly, it was quite fun."

She then proceeds to tell us for a good 15 minutes how cool it is to stay in one place while flying with a drone to a completely different one.

"When we were still in training, Memphis suggested we make a competition out of it and race with our drones. I assume you can guess how it ended."

"Badly?" I ask, smiling.

"Well, you can certainly consider crashing a pretty valuable drone into a tree at full speed a bad ending."

We all laugh at that. It honestly must be cool to serve with your partner or best friend. Why do I not have that?

For a moment I feel like asking for a post with some of my friends, but then I remember I'm reckless enough to want to go to the front.

"There's also one thing that sounds stupid, but it pains me beyond imagining that I have Memphis by my side almost at all times and don't have time to be with him at all." Grace's face turns sad. "But well, at least he's near, and we work together sometimes. I can't imagine being there alone. How do you cope with that, Lorna?"

"Oh, it's fine," I say. "I have an amazing captain, and everyone seems to be more or less nice," I smile.

"So, what do you do?" Grace asks.

"I was operating an air defense complex," I say proudly. It does sound cool.

I tell them about the specifics of my post and about the people I've met there.

"Did you like it?" asks Ruby.

"It was pretty cool, but got a little boring with time. I want to go to the frontline after the break." I catch the stunned faces of my friends as I say this.

Silence hangs in the air for a moment before Grace breaks it. "What?" she almost whispers. "Aren't you scared?"

I am, I guess. Fuck it, of course I am. But I still want it. "I'll figure it out when I get to it." I smile.

I know my friends – especially Grace – worry about me, but I can't do anything about it. I'll survive at my new post though, I know. I'll figure it out when I get to it, just like I always have.

CHAPTER 30

SWEET 21

I open my eyes and hear birds sing. I get up and open the window to let the sound and the rays of the morning sun in. It's still sunrise. The sky is painted green and blue, and a couple of pink clouds lazily float across it. Seems like a good start of the day. I stare out of the window for a little longer and then go drink blood before training. Even though now we can train when we feel like it, I still wake up early.

At the gym, I meet with Grace, Roy, and Memphis. Just like good old *peaceful* times.

"Hey birthday girl! How are you feeling?!" Grace screams and hugs me so tightly I can barely breathe.

"I'm good," I manage. "How do you know it's my birthday?" I ask.

She rolls her eyes. "You said it yourself when we played truth or dare. Don't you remember?"

"I do, I guess, I just never thought *you* remembered it," I say, smiling. It's good when your friends remember about your birthday after all.

"Of course we did," says Memphis and hugs me. "Happy 21." He nudges Roy with an elbow.

"Ah, happy birthday," Roy says and gives me a box.

"We were thinking for quite a long time and decided that the present should remind you of us or it's not really interesting," comments Memphis.

I open the box and see a pendant. A snake. It's so sweet they even remember my favorite animal. I laugh and say, "And who exactly should it remind me of?"

"Actually," says Grace through laughter, "we made it ourselves. Memphis made the snake, I made the rope. And Roy made the pattern on the snake, that's why it's crooked."

"Hey," says Roy with mock offense and pushes Grace's shoulder, and she laughs even harder, almost losing her balance.

"It's amazing," I say and hug the three of them.

Roy suggested we fight today, so I pair up with Memphis. "So what are you waiting for?" I say, raising my eyebrows.

"For an opportunity," he says slowly and makes a few careful steps toward me, his whole body tense.

"Opportunity for what?" I ask casually, my body relaxed.

"For this," he says and swings his hand, aiming for my shoulder. I grab it and twist. I kick his legs, and he falls.

I laugh. "You really thought I didn't guess?"

"I hoped," he says, laughing too. He swings his leg to kick me, but I just jump over it. It was too obvious he would do that.

"You're too predictable, you know that?" I say as he gets up.

"Oh, you sound like Arthur." He rolls his eyes. I just shrug.

"Okay, try to predict that," he says and walks past me and leaves the fighting ring, leaving me there, stunned. Was he offended by my words? I turn my head in the direction he went to and get punched in the jaw. I take a few steps back before I regain my balance. That was indeed unpredictable.

He smiles at me and tries to punch me again. This time I'm prepared, so I block and aim for his stomach. He dodges and gets behind me. Without turning, I kick in his general direction with my leg. Then I turn, swinging my hand, and it meets his face. I hear a crack.

Memphis clutches his nose with both hands. Oh shit, I must've broken it.

Grace runs to the ring, Roy close on her heels. Memphis sits on the floor, blood streaming down his hands.

"I'm so sorry," I say. It's a stupid thing to say on such occasions, but there's nothing else I can do.

He makes an okay sign with his hand and mutters, "I'll live."

"We should go to the hospital," says Grace, and I nod. She and Roy help Memphis to his feet, and we leave the gym.

In the hospital, we meet Eric. His arm is bandaged, the bandage red from blood. While guys go into the doctor's office with Memphis, I stay in the hallway.

"What happened to your hand?" I ask.

"Just one of those stupid challenges I do with friends. I fell off a bike. You can join us sometime if you want, by the way."

"Oh, I'm always up for a stupid challenge," I say, giggling. "Really. I'd love to join."

"Good." He winks at me. "What happened to your friend?" he asks.

I bite my lip. "I punched him."

"Oh, had an argument?" he asks.

"*No*, no. Just training." I can't really imagine arguing with my friends to the extent that I will punch one of them in the nose.

He nods. "Anyway, I'll see you around," he says.

"Yeah, have a nice day."

He's nice. I think we might even become friends at some point. A thought crosses my mind. If things were different and he really was our instructor — as I first assumed — how possible is it that I would have fallen for him? I smile at my thoughts. Does he have a partner? What's he like in a relationship? In bed? I shake my head to get rid of all those ridiculous thoughts.

Just then the door opens and my friends walk out — Memphis has some kind of a cast on his nose — followed by, "Stay out of your stupid fights," from the doctor.

"Isn't she the sweetest?" I can't keep from commenting.

"You probably come here so often you already hate each other," jokes Memphis.

"We hated each other from the very first sight," I say. Damn, do they really think I come here at least *sometimes*?

"Well, enough training for me today. I think I need some rest," says Memphis, laughing a little.

"Again, I'm so sorry. Really," I say, embarrassed.

"It's ok. Don't worry," he assures me. "I think it's actually good that we can break each other's noses, and no one is offended."

"Indeed." I laugh. "Okay, see ya. Get well soon," I say and leave them.

I walk to my room, humming some song to myself. Apparently, I'm in a very good mood even despite today's events. I don't notice when I even start dancing until I bump into someone.

"Oh, sorry," I mutter and lift my head to look who the poor thing is. It seems I stepped on their foot.

"Someone's in a good mood?" Arthur asks, and instead of answering, I just kiss him. After we break from each other, I smile at him.

"Come to my room a little later," he says and walks away. Usually I would think about what I did wrong, but today I don't care at all, so I just continue dancing down the hallway.

I knock on Arthur's door.

"Open," I hear, and as I enter, I see Arthur coming to me, his silhouette merging with shadows because of the black clothes he wears. He extends his hand. "A dance?"

I raise an eyebrow, confused, but take his hand anyway. Music starts playing as he pulls me closer to him. First, I put my hand on his shoulder, but after a couple of seconds, I wrap my arms around his waist and lay my head on his shoulder instead. We stand there in the semidarkness, swaying to the rhythm.

On such moments, it seems like there's nothing but the two of us in this world – no wars, no violence, no fear. I lose myself in his smell, his touch. He is all I could wish for. A partner, a family, a soulmate.

I turn my head to bury my face in his neck to keep from crying. In the world that's crashing down, where it seems like there's nothing left, I have him to hold on to.

Our relationship would seem so strange to other people. We can lie in bed for hours, talking about the most personal things, and we can not communicate for days. Maybe it's really strange, but I'm fine with that. I think we both are.

In a while, he says, "Hey, it's your birthday after all. I have something for you."

"You know?"

"Of course I do." He gives me a long, narrow box.

"What's in there?" I ask.

"There's only one way to find out." He grins.

So I open it. I gasp when I see what's inside.

Black hilt with the letter L made with black gemstones on it. Blade made of perfect silver, perfectly sharp. I slide my hand on it, admiring the sword. I'm mesmerized.

"Thank you," I say in complete awe. "It's amazing."

Arthur just smiles back at me.

"I really can't wait to try it, but I think it can wait until tomorrow," I say and kiss him. "Now I probably have something better to do. If you don't mind."

"You're choosing me over a sword? I'm impressed," he says, laughing, and that makes me laugh too.

"Only this once," I say.

"Okay," he says thoughtfully. "Do you trust me?"

"With what?" I ask, confused.

He goes to the table and takes a piece of black cloth from it. He shows it to me as if asking, and I nod.

He steps behind me and covers my eyes. The fabric is soft against my skin. Arthur puts his hands on my shoulders and leads me somewhere. I giggle at the thought of how ridiculous I must look trying to walk normally.

"Ready?" he asks, his voice low and steady.

"I think." I smile. He takes the cloth off my eyes, and my jaw drops in surprise.

"Damn, it's…" is all I manage. I take in my surroundings. There's no light in his room, except for candles – black as the room's interior to which I thought I already got used to. But in this light, it looks different somehow. On the floor and the bed, there are petals of black roses. It all looks like a gothic altar. "That's awesome," I say.

I want to turn to face him, but before I do, he slips his arms around my waist, kissing my neck. I close my eyes to concentrate on the feelings. I turn my head and kiss him on the lips.

With a graceful, effortless move, he turns me to face him, lifts me up and throws me onto the bed. He stands above me like a statue for a couple of seconds before pulling off his T-shirt. I thought I got used to him, and I really did, but he still seems perfect to me. I can stare at his body for hours.

He gets on top of me and puts his elbows on both sides of my body, our eyes locked. Damn, that color. Is it normal that he's all I have on my mind now? Does he think of me the way I think of him?

I put my hand on his cheek, a small smile on my lips. All I want now is to lock us in this room, to feel him all over me. His touch on my skin, his voice in my ear, his eyes looking into my soul.

I slide my hand to his neck. His mine. Only mine.

"You could have any girl you want? Why me?"

He snorts. "Do I really have to answer this question?"

"Why not?" I say.

"Because it's ridiculous."

I raise my eyebrows at his comment. "I've already told you so many times about what I like in you. And well, you don't choose who to love, so I was just lucky I fell for you." He pauses. "By the way, if *you* could choose, would it be me?"

I laugh. "Probably not," I say and immediately add, "Not. Until I knew the real you. You know, the image you show to trainees sucks."

He laughs again. "I know. I know it does," he says and kisses me, sliding his arm under my sweatshirt to my ribs. Then he slides down again and takes the knife out of my pants sling and puts it on the bed next to me.

I raise my eyebrows in a silent question, but Arthur ignores it. He takes off my pants and my underwear, leaving me in my sweatshirt. He traces with his hand up my inner thigh and brushes my clit lightly. I gasp.

Arthur grips the back of my neck and lifts me off the bed toward him. I put my hand on his forearm and look into his sky-blue eyes. He grins and takes off my sweatshirt and bra. Then he pushes me back so I lie down again.

"Do you trust me?" he asks again.

"With my life," I say honestly.

He picks up the knife that was lying beside me and traces from my collarbone to the space between my breasts, barely touching the skin. Then he switches his attention to my arm and cuts it. I twitch a little from surprise.

"Does it hurt?" Arthur whispers.

"It's fine."

"I didn't ask if it was fine or not. I asked, *does it hurt?*" he repeats with an edge to his voice.

"No, it doesn't," I breathe out.

Arthur nods and cuts once more. Pleasant tingles run through me as he traces the knife down my arm, right to my wrist. I look at my arm and see the red line.

He keeps cutting me all over, occasionally leaning down to lick the blood off me or to plant a few kisses in-between the cuts. My whole body burns. I wouldn't even notice the pain if there were only a few cuts. But with my body now lined with red stripes, I can feel it clearly. It hurts so good, I'm crazy enough to enjoy it.

He stops under my left breast to leave quite a few cuts there. As I concentrate on the feeling, I realize those aren't just cuts. They're letters.

I rise on my elbow to look at the place. I see *'Arthur'* in blood-red lines.

"What the hell are you doing?" I ask, smiling.

"Marking you as mine?" he answers and licks his 'masterpiece.'

I just lie back down to let him do whatever he wants. This mark will fade soon enough, anyway. *Make it permanent*, my heart screams at me. *Ask him to make it permanent!* But I restrain myself.

We both jumped into this relationship headfirst and gave it all we had, but that's too soon. That's something way too strong. I want it, damn, I want it so bad, but we can do it any time. So I bite my lip and concentrate on the feelings to not think of that anymore.

When he's done playing with me, Arthur pulls me to him so I lie on his chest and stare out of the window at the night city. I'm slightly disappointed that he didn't even fuck me, but it's so good to just be near him. He brushes his fingers over my temple. When he starts speaking, his voice is low and soft. "Do you like the way things are? With us."

"What do you mean?" I say.

"I mean, we've just had not only a great time but time valuable for us both, I believe, and it is more than likely I won't hear from you in the next couple of days."

Fuck. Seems like this way was comfortable only for me. "You know, I'm fine with that," I say honestly.

Arthur sits up and blankly stares out of the window. I rise on my elbow and stare at his back, not knowing what to say. We sit like that for a minute before he gets up and walks out of the room, murmuring, "Fine."

At first, I'm just confused. Then I want to follow him, then not to. I really don't know what to do.

Maybe I really shouldn't be comfortable with such a way? Well, I do want to spend more time with him, it's just... just too complicated.

After a couple of minutes, I get up from the bed and walk out of the bedroom. The living room is empty, and it makes me nervous. Then I notice Arthur on the balcony. Awkwardly, I walk toward him.

"Hey," I say, my voice more quiet than I expected. I clear my throat. "Don't you think we need to talk?" I say a little too accusingly.

"I'm sorry, I freaked out," he says without turning to me. I come closer and stand near him at the railing, the night air cold against my naked body. "You know, I just want to spend more time with you so much I didn't even think of how you feel," he adds.

"I want it too," I admit. "To spend more time with you, I mean."

He looks at me. "What's the problem then?" he asks a little too harshly, frustration lacing his voice.

"I... I don't know," I stutter. "It just feels like the more I dive into a relationship, the more I lose freedom. It's crazy, I know."

"It's not," he says. "I understand this feeling completely."

I stare at him wide-eyed. "You do?"

He nods. "I just want you to know that I'm not limiting your freedom. No way."

"I know," I interrupt him. "I know. It's not about us, not about *our* relationship." He raises his eyebrows questioningly. "It's just a general feeling. Maybe I'm afraid of obligations, I don't know." I shrug.

"No obligations." He smiles softly. "Really. Neither of us is obliged to anything. We're together as long as we both want it. And each of us does only what they see fit. Right?"

"Right." I nod and smile. It's good that he feels this way. I hug him. "I love you," I say.

"I love you too, Rebel," he answers.

I close my eyes. I can't get enough of this feeling. He's just so... home.

"I have something else for you," he says and hands me a pendant. It looks like a crystal filled with some red liquid.

Wait, what? I stare at him without blinking.

"You..." I mean to say something, but I don't know what.

"Yes. I'm forever yours. I love you," he says, and I hug him tightly, still in disbelief.

It's a rather ancient tradition. Almost no one does it these days. If someone is in love and they want to show that they belong to the other person, they fill a piece of jewelry – most commonly a pendant – with their blood and give it to their loved one. It's meant to say, *'I'm forever yours, so I'm giving you a part of me.'* And if the receiving person accepts, they kind of answer, *'I accept your love and you to be mine.'* It can be considered an equivalent of human marriage. Except marriage is two-sided, and this can be one-sided.

It must hurt so much. To give yourself to someone only to realize that they either don't want you at all or agree to have you, but don't give themselves back. It seems like a huge risk to take.

I definitely accept Arthur's love, and I definitely want to give the same in return.

CHAPTER 31

WRONG

I'm back on the battlefield. Arthur wasn't very happy about my ambition to be on the frontline, but I told him that letting me do that is the only way I won't do anything stupid. I don't think I've convinced him, though. I know *I'm* not convinced.

Being directly engaged with the enemy turned out to be less scary than I thought. I've become pretty confident in combat, and the hours and hours I devoted to perfecting my sword skills do show.

Battles are becoming more fierce, but each time I hold the sword Arthur gave me, I feel more powerful. I feel like I can't lose while I have it.

I haven't been home in a while. I start missing my room... and the carefree time we had once. The time when I didn't know how explosions sounded or even further, when I didn't know how to fire a gun. Maybe I should've stayed with my mom and live like she says. Sometimes I feel like just leave it all, let it all be. I'm tired.

But I can't stop, not anymore. I've gone too far. I'll fight. I'll fight until I die.

I put on my armor, pull my hair into a ponytail, grab my sword, and leave the tent. Time to give some hell.

Today, our mission is to eradicate the enemy camp. We're walking through the trees, a few kilometers to the side of the camp to avoid detection. *Trees* is an overstatement, though. As I walk, all I see is sticks jutting out from the ground. They don't even have leaves anymore. There's smoke all around me, and the world looks grey despite the sun. Burned. Lifeless. Destroyed.

How vibrant this forest must have been before the war came. Animals running around doing their animal things. Plants growing near water streams. The sun and the moon covering the beauty in their glow.

I step over yet another burned log and tears well up in my eyes. We aren't just destroying ourselves, we're killing the planet. And there's nothing, *nothing* I can do to stop this. Because if I lay down my arms, I will just let Vivian's people destroy everything. And if I don't...

If I don't, I might have a chance to protect at least a piece of that beauty.

We emerge right behind the camp. The sound of explosions makes me involuntarily startle from time to time. The sounds here are worse than I've ever heard. But the weird thing is I can't say I'm scared. I mean, I am, but not more than usual.

Nearing the camp, we split up to surround them. An enemy soldier spots us, but it's too late for them. I get into a sword fight with one of them, and I can't help but notice how much my skills have improved. I win with almost no effort.

I look around and see that no one is fighting anymore, and the enemy soldiers are all dead. I don't think any of us are even tired, let alone injured. It's weird.

"Am I missing something?" I ask no one in particular. A louder explosion follows my words.

"Job's done, time to get back," says the leader of the mission, and we head for the tree line. I stay behind, ignoring the order to follow. I focus on the sounds around me. Or more so, the absence of any sound.

I've learned it's normal for a battlefield to be silent, nature either dead or gone. But something is wrong. Something is very wrong.

"I think we should stay here and plan," I call out to my team.

"Stop being paranoid, Lorna," an older soldier barks, turning to me. "Let's go."

"No," I say and take a step back reflexively. "No. It's a mistake. A big mistake." Panic creeps into my blood. I have no idea what it is, but I feel it with every cell of my body. This is *wrong*.

"Tell everyone to come back out right now!" I command.

He doesn't have time to respond as an explosion sounds. But this time it's not distant, it's right in front of me, right in the tree line.

I drop to the ground immediately, covering my head with my hands as parts of trees and dirt rain down on me. I hear screams, or maybe I'm hallucinating.

I lie on the ground as explosions continue for at least a good 5 minutes. When the sound dies down, I dare to lift my head to see the dead tree line – what's left of it – on fire.

I stare at the flames, realizing what a huge mistake it was even coming here. My unit for the mission had 10 people. Now it has one.

I come as close to the forest as I dare and scream, "Is anyone alive?" in hopes someone will answer. But they don't. My gaze settles on a limb just a few meters from me. A *fucking limb!*

I turn to the camp. Four of their soldiers down in exchange for our nine. So not worth it.

This was a trap. It was a trap all along. To get us here. To make us think we weren't in danger. To make us think we could win this.

But it's not that thought that makes my skin crawl with goosebumps and the panic rise even more. It's the realization that they sacrificed four of their people to make this trap possible.

As I hike back to where we left our vehicles, I roll the thought over and over in my head. This is ridiculous. That doesn't make any sense. I don't think Vivian is above sacrificing her people left and right, but that was just not worth it. She killed nine of our people, and they objectively weren't our best fighters. Why would she go to such lengths as to blow up a damn forest to kill nine or, like she probably intended, ten of us? She isn't stupid enough to think we'd take more people on such a mission. None of this makes sense, something is very wrong here. I just don't yet know what.

CHAPTER 32

OVER

Today, Arthur came to our camp. He visits different divisions from time to time and fights alongside us. He's absolutely worthy of being the leader, I have no doubt about that.

He told us that Vivian has been developing a new chemical weapon for a while. At least that's what our sources say, though I don't know what the sources are.

We need to infiltrate a laboratory where they work on the chemical. Ideally, we are to take samples and research data so that we can research it too and develop an antidote. We must do that stealthily and without being noticed so that they don't even know we were there.

I wondered why not simply destroy everything, but when I asked Arthur, he explained that destroying the lab doesn't guarantee that they don't have the information elsewhere as well. But researching it ourselves and making the antidote while letting them think they have a thing against us can give us an advantage. And honestly, I agree. That's smart. I probably wouldn't think of that, I'm too impulsive.

There's also a part of me that wants to do them some visible damage *right now*. But I'll hold it back since not doing so would be a stupid move. If the mission goes sideways, though, we are to destroy the lab with all the data.

We split into three teams. Each is responsible for one level of the facility. On my team are me, Abigail – who transferred to my division not so long ago – and a guy that I've never met named Andy. Though now that I think of it, I saw him around the camp a few times.

When we're at the spot, I look around and all I see is endless fields. There's not a sign of any military object. There's no sign of anything at all.

I knew the lab is underground, but I instantly note how different it is from Vivian's usual locations. I've always found it weird that her soldiers don't hide much. All their camps are too easy to locate and their bases too easy to destroy. This place isn't like that. If I didn't know better, I would've never guessed this place is anything but a field.

We walk to the middle of the field and I don't think I've ever felt that exposed. Arthur squats and I see a panel on the ground next to him as he punches in a code.

The ground shifts, and a hatch opens, revealing the stairs. Arthur's team goes in first since they have the lowest level, then goes the other team and only then us, since we're responsible for the highest level.

We climb down and as soon as my feet hit the ground, I hold my sword ready. We walk through the blue hallways until we encounter a guard – who we have to kill and lock the body in a closet we find. By the time his comrades find him, we'll be long gone.

We check all the rooms we pass, but none have what we came for. We avoid a few other guards, but I notice that there are no scientists. I know that Arthur and his right hand choose the time carefully, but it still doesn't sit well with me. The facility can't be that empty at any hour. I feel a rush of déjà vu at these thoughts. Something is *fucking wrong!*

We get to the last but one room and find a wall of samples and a row of computers.

"That's what we need," Abigail whispers. I nod, and we get inside.

"Work fast and leave," Andy reminds us, his hazel eyes devoid of any emotion.

I go straight to the computers to look for data. I get all the files that seem at least remotely useful to me on the portable data holder I have.

I can't help but delete a few files that are already on the data holder from the computer. Files get lost sometimes, don't they?

Suddenly, the alarm blares, and in a moment footsteps and voices are heard down the hallway.

"Retreat," Andy orders, and I grab the data holder. I hope I managed to get at least something useful.

Andy quickly does something with the wires, starting a fire. We run into the hallway, and Abigail throws a grenade inside, destroying the lab completely.

Three guards come at us, and we each engage one. I kill mine with a sword to the chest before helping Abigail out of the chokehold another one had on her.

We run to the stairs and get outside, where a few dozen soldiers wait. That can't be a coincidence or a fast reaction. They knew we'd come. We get into fighting.

In some time, the second-level team joins us. Third-level one is nowhere to be seen.

Even outnumbered, our people are more skilled than Vivian's, so when they realize we're winning, they retreat, still showering us with bullets as they run to their vehicles. *Fuck, I should've tried to destroy the vehicles.*

I aim at one of the soldiers with my gun and fire, hitting her shoulder. The asshole will live, but I hope she at least remembers me.

One of the soldiers throws a knife. Last breath in this battle. I trace with my eyes where it will fly and notice Abigail – who's still fighting with another enemy soldier – right at its trajectory.

Everything around me seems to slow as I spin my options in my head. Warn her? She's too busy to pay me attention. Just let whatever happens happen? It will kill her.

I run a few meters to my left to block the stab with my body. Whatever happens – happens. I can't let my friend die.

Just when I enter the knife's trajectory, seeing it fly right at me, I feel arms wrap around my waist, and someone pulls me with them. We both fall to the ground. Despite the haze in my eyes, I recognize the arms as Arthur's.

"No!" I scream as I see the knife land right at the back of Abigail's neck. You don't survive such wounds.

I see her limp body fall to the ground, lifeless, and try to move toward her, but Arthur just holds me tighter.

"Let me go," I half scream and try to break free. I don't know why I'm doing this. I know I can't help her now. But still, I try to free myself from Arthur's grip.

"Let me go!" I scream again, hysterically this time, and kick his arm.

"Let me go," I say and start crying, my body goes limp, and I cover my face with my hands.

Arthur loosens his hold on me, and I stand up immediately. I take a couple of steps away from him and then turn around.

"What the hell?! Why the hell did you do that?! I could've saved her!" I shout at him, my anger rising.

"No, you would've died," he says back calmly.

"It doesn't matter what could happen to me. *She* could have lived."

He inhales to say something, but I don't let him. "Why do you always do that? Why do you always have to '*protect*' me?" I say as I remember all those times Arthur would try to keep me out of harm's way. *'Don't get too involved in a battle.' 'Stay far from explosions.' 'Don't be too reckless.'* This time his protectiveness cost my friend her life.

"I never asked for this. *Why?*" I demand hysterically, tears falling from my eyes.

"I think I can let myself have a little bit of selfishness. I don't want you *dead.*" He raises his voice at the last sentence.

"Don't come any close to me. Ever," I blurt out without fully realizing what I say. I see his gaze shift from anger to confusion, then fear, then emptiness.

"So be it," he says and walks away.

Tears dry on my cheeks. I stare at his back, and if a gaze could burn, I swear he'd be in flames by now.

We gather at the meeting spot in the cover of a few trees that grow around the field to return to the camp. Arthur asks, "What casualties do we have?"

A few people say they're wounded, one guy unconscious but alive. Abigail's face appears in my mind's eye. At least I don't have to be the one to say it. He knows already.

I don't say a word during the ride back, and in my tent I just fall on my bed, exhausted more emotionally than physically. A picture of Abigail flashes before my eyes once more, and tears roll down my cheeks. It's good that my tent-mate is on some other mission and I'm alone now.

I was so close to saving my friend. Just a couple more seconds. If only Arthur didn't stop me. She could have lived. She *would* have lived. I feel such anger and hatred towards what he did, towards his sudden habit of always protecting me. Why does he have to decide what I do? It's none of his business, even if we're dating. I close my eyes and try to calm down and just breathe. *In-out, in-out.*

And suddenly I feel so lonely. I have to go through all of this alone. Again. I want his arms around me. His comforting voice telling me that it's going to be alright. But what's done is done. It's over. We're over.

I roll to the side and try to fall asleep as my pillow becomes wet with my tears. I've lost it. I'm an idiot.

The next morning I decide to train a little since I have a day off. My mood is to punch someone or something, so I just end up punching a tree until my knuckles become scratched and bruised. Then I turn to some knife throwing. Poor tree.

Yesterday, I felt so sad and lonely but now I feel only anger. Towards this situation, towards this war. All this mess. And I think that my emotions should be different considering the situation. I try to look deeper inside myself to try to find some sorrow, pity, remorse, sadness, any humane feeling. But I can't find anything, I don't feel it.

It's not sad, it's scary. War is not sad, it doesn't make me cry or get into depression. It only makes me angry. It makes me want to put a bullet into the heads of those who just kill others without thinking. It makes me want to kill myself because I'm no different now. How many lives have I taken and didn't even acknowledge it? Enemy lives, but lives nonetheless. When did I become so ruthless, so inhumane?

War can reveal the worst and the best in us. The worst war can do to us is to make us like the ones we fight against. We have to focus on keeping the good things we have in us or otherwise, what's the point?

I'll feel this terrible for a while more, but eventually, this feeling will pass. I know that eventually every bad thing will pass. I'm experienced enough to know that by now. I just have to wait.

CHAPTER 33

TOO BLIND TO SEE

I lie on my bunk bed, my eyes closed. I can't fall asleep because of all the recent events. I hear a blow, the ground starts shaking violently. It's closer than before. Too close. They're getting closer to the camps, to the castle.

Another one. I hear the faint sound of a plane flying. My heart starts racing. Is it that bad? They're just gonna bomb us while we sleep?

Battling is one thing, but bombs is a completely different one. You can't do anything about them. You're helpless. It's just up to a chance.

I take deep breaths to calm down. In a few minutes, it helps.

Then I hear a plane again. Too loud. Too close. It seems like it flies right above my head, but I understand that, of course, it doesn't. The understanding doesn't make it less scary, though.

Another one. This time louder and for a longer period. I clutch Arthur's pendant – I still have it with me at all times despite what happened between us – in my hand. As I feel its sleek surface and the faint lines of his name engraved on it, I feel safer. I understand that it won't protect me, but I don't care.

I hear the sound of a plane again. I chant in my head, *fly past the tent fly past the tent fly past the tent*. Too scared a bomb will fall right at me. A blow. A shake. I gasp. It's worse than before. For a second, I think the tent is going to collapse.

Another plane. *Fly past the tent fly past the tent fly past the tent.* A blow somewhere in the distance. My heart feels as if it's being squeezed and my lungs don't get enough air.

And again. *Fly past the tent fly past tent!* I scream hysterically in my head, my fingers wrapped around the pendant so tight it hurts. A blow louder than I've ever heard, the shaking is longer and more violent. I see a flash outside, too bright.

I've never been so scared in my life. Although it's ridiculous how your fears change. During the first days of war, I was terrified of the slightest noise, and now a blow like this causes the same amount of fear. Maybe you just become numb with time. Or maybe new fears just get so big you don't pay attention to the former ones.

Everything seems to calm down for now, and a memory from my childhood invades my mind. I don't remember how old I was, but for sure, less than six. We were returning home from a friend and heard a plane. My mom pointed at the sky and said it was a warplane. I loved watching the occasional planes fly when I was a child, but that time there was something besides joy. Something overwhelming, something dark. I didn't know it then, but now I do. It was anxiety, panic for no reason – my first time ever feeling this.

It seemed like time had stopped. Only darkness around, and the only thing my eyes saw was the plane, which, as if in slow motion, drifted across the sky.

I felt terrified then and didn't know why. I could never imagine that in about 15 years I'll hear these planes fly literally above my head, carrying bombs to drop them just a few kilometers away. I think sometimes life tells us about what's to happen, but most of the time we're too blind to see, too stupid to grasp, too rational to believe. I wish I'd considered it to be a warning. Not that I could've done anything, but maybe, just maybe, I would have.

CHAPTER 34

AUTOMATIC

Just another day of battles, bloodshed, and suffering. I've lost count of how long it's been going on. My moves are automatic, my mind numb. Just onwards and forwards day after day. Receive a task, prepare, perform. Don't think, just do.

Sometimes a part of me that's still alive awakens and I feel things, but I get less and less of that.

"In positions!" booms my captain's voice.

Without overthinking why, I run to my post. I jump into the trench and run to my weapon, standing there waiting for me. Before I reach it, the ground shakes, and I lose my balance for a moment, almost face-planting the dirt but catching myself in time.

At my position, I risk a peek outside and see artillery raining on us. The ground keeps shaking, but I steady myself and aim for their complexes.

The worst thing about these weapons is that they launch multiple shells at the same time with no target whatsoever. Just a general direction. They're nowhere near as deadly in terms of firepower as rockets and bombs, but you also never see them coming until it's too late.

I keep my focus on my opponents, managing to shoot one complex. A victory, however very small. A pained scream rips me out of my short triumph. A chill runs down my spine. A reminder that every day we lose our people. But more than that, people lose their partners, their children, their parents, their friends. I hate that. And every time I take a life, I can't help but think about that too.

When the ordeal is over and I get out of the trench, I see the ground littered with shells. They stick out of the dirt like metal trees. Substitution for the real ones they – we – destroyed long ago. I see a puddle of blood next to one shell. So much. Too much. I keep walking.

I hear a moan and rush to help a wounded soldier. When I near her, a blow sounds. The bomb lands only about 50 meters away from me, judging by the deafening sound.

I turn and see a huge ball of light. It blinds me for a second. A bang still loud in my ears. And then the time stops.

As if in slow motion, wind blows and light spreads all around me. A wave of heat hits me, and I feel my skin starting to burn. If I were still human, I'd already be dead. But I just stand there, almost at the epicenter, watching my skin turn to ashes, the wind blowing it away. I feel neither pain nor fear. My eyes are glued to the growing light. Then a wave hits me, and I fly what seems like a couple of dozen meters in a flash. I hit my head and fade into the black.

I open my eyes and see the white walls of the hospital. The castle hospital. How long have I been out? My body burns so much I don't even try to get up. It seems I'm alone in the room, so it's fine. I stare at the ceiling for a while and then fall back asleep.

When I wake up, I feel better. My wounds started to heal. I get up to leave the room but stop, thinking that I probably should tell the doctor that I'm leaving. I have no idea why I decided to do that. But I wait for her, anyway.

She comes in about half an hour. The first thing she says is, "I see you too often."

It would be much more often if I went here every time I should. "How can I address you?" I ask, realizing I don't even know her name.

"Dr. Brink," she says. I nod in acknowledgement.

"How long have I been out?" I ask.

"Two days." My eyes round in surprise. "You were hurt pretty badly. If the soldiers got to you later, you'd be dead," she says.

Two days... My friends must be losing their minds. That if they even know. Does Arthur know?

"Well, thank you for the treatment, I'll go now," I say, getting up. Before she can say anything, I add, "I won't fight until I heal. I'll be in my room." I shut the door behind me.

On the way to my room, I stop and stare out of the window for a while. All I see is darkness and the stillness of the night. At the distance, I hear battle. Even from this far, it seems fierce.

I already start walking when I see an explosion on the horizon. A ball of light shines in the night sky. Relatively small at first, but growing bigger with each second. It seems like the light is all that's left alive. I watch it, mesmerized as it grows. It looks like the sun is rising, engulfing everything with its shine. It could've been beautiful if it wasn't so deadly. I hear a blow, and the walls shake a little. Then the light disappears and smoke replaces it. What was that? And what damage can something so powerful do? I hope no one suffered from it. I just hope all my friends are fine.

I walk down the hallway when I suddenly start feeling dizzy. I sway and put my hands on the wall to steady myself, and then I hear ringing. I realize it's in my head. Faint at first, but getting louder fast. Soon it deafens all the sounds of the real world.

Along with the sound, my vision blackens. I shake my head, but it doesn't help. Panic takes over me. What do I do now? Is it the end? I feel like I'm falling into the void, but try to grab onto something, anyway.

A few more seconds of panic and desperation, and the ringing gradually stops. I shake my head one more time to make sure. What the hell was that? Maybe I should've stayed at the hospital after all.

CHAPTER 35

DARE TO FORGIVE

Because of my pretty severe injuries, Dr. Brink instructed that I don't go on missions for at least a week, so I stay at the castle. But it doesn't mean I can't have fun.

Today, Eric invited me to do some craziness with him and his friends. I love that even during the war people still manage to have fun. I understand that it's possible for everyone to have quite a lot of days off only because our army is way bigger than that of Vivian and they mostly use long-distance weapons anyway, so no point in having all of us on the battlefield. But still, not everyone can just let go and have fun at times like this.

We meet near the train tracks. When I come, Eric and a couple of his friends are already there.

"So, that's Lorna?" a girl with a pink death hawk and lots of tattoos asks. Eric nods. I extend my hand, and she shakes it.

"I'm Avery," she says, her voice much lower than you expect a female voice to be.

"That's Andy." Eric points to a man standing a couple steps away, looking at the distance, and I instantly remember him from the lab mission. The lab mission... I block the thought.

"Um, hi," I say. Now that we're in a more peaceful environment, I notice how silky his black hair looks as it almost envelopes his face, hiding his cheekbones from view. His hazel eyes look calm now.

"Ah, never mind him," says Avery, rolling her eyes. "He's not the talkative type. Sometimes it really pisses me off."

I snort. "Are we waiting for anyone else?" I ask.

"Yeah. Alina, Skylar, and," Eric looks at Avery, "Is Blake coming?"

"He'll meet us on the train," she says.

"Then just two more. Oh, here they are."

I turn my head and smile when I see Sky. I come to her and hug her.

"Hey, Eric didn't mention you'd be here today," she says.

"Surprise!" I laugh.

"That's my sister, Alina," says Skylar. I extend my hand, and the girl tugs at her shoulder-length brown hair, hesitating, but shakes it anyway. The shake is too awkward, weak, and uncomfortable.

"She's just not used to such ways," Sky says, and I frown but keep silent.

"The train is coming," announces Andy, breaking the silence. His voice is low, and he speaks slowly, like he's just woken up.

"Do we... jump?" I assume, suddenly realizing we're not near the station. Eric just smiles at me, and I understand it's a yes.

I stare at the train coming toward us, thinking of how I should pull this 'stunt' off, especially with my injuries still healing. *That's ridiculous,* I say to myself and smile.

The train rides past us, and we start running with it. Eric is the first to jump. He grabs the handle and throws himself inside. Avery and Andy are next.

I notice the handle near me and grab it. The force of the train drags me with it, and I push myself off the ground, jumping on the train. I see Skylar pulling Alina inside, and when we're all on the train, I say, "So, I guess it's just the beginning, huh?"

"You bet," rings a voice from the other side of the car.

"Blake!" shrieks Avery and jumps into the guy's arms. Even in the dim light of the car, I can see that his body is covered with tattoos. His hair is long and dark, the sides shaven. He lifts her off the floor to his shoulder. She giggles.

Still hanging from his shoulder, Avery says, "The girl's Lorna. Eric mentioned."

He nods at me. "Welcome to the crazy."

I smile. "Thanks."

I sit near the edge of the car and look at the fast-changing scenery the war hasn't changed yet. I should probably be afraid, but I'm not. I trust my hands to hold me steady on the moving train. I think my brain just refuses the danger.

"Ready to jump?" asks Eric from behind. I get up and nod.

We are moving past rocky cliffs just near the sea when Eric shouts, "Now!" and jumps out. Without hesitation, I do the same. My hands let go of the handles, my legs pushing me out. I land on the rocky ground and fall on one knee. It hurts a little, but I manage to keep my balance. I see that Eric noticed my fall, but he just smiles lightly at me, like nothing happened.

"So, I'm sure you know truth or dare. Well, what we do here is basically a dare. Anything crazy or weird is a way to go," says Eric, and I nod. "Usually it happens like this. Hey Andy, I dare you to sing a song," he shouts, grinning.

"Eric, really?" asks Andy, defeated. "You know I can't sing."

"That's why." Eric giggles. Andy rolls his eyes and starts singing. I wish he never did. It sounds awful.

"For how long does he have to do this?" I ask, cringing.

"Up to him," replies Eric. I look at Andy, and it doesn't seem like he's about to stop. He seems to enjoy it.

"Maybe enough?" I say, and everyone laughs.

"Really, don't torture the girl from the beginning. She's not used to your mewling," comments Avery.

"It wasn't *my* idea," snaps Andy.

We move closer to the edge of the cliff, laughing and daring each other to do stupid things.

"Eric, Lorna, I dare you to kiss," says Andy. I look at Eric. Will he say anything?

"So?" he asks, looking back at me. I just shrug. I don't know what to answer. I would just do that, but I don't know how Eric will react to such straightforwardness. So instead of acting, I stop myself. It looks like I'm afraid, though I'm not. I hate that.

"You can opt out if you want to, you know," he says.

"No," I say a little too sharply. "I mean, it's a game, right? Let's play it then." I feel stupid.

"Okay." He smiles and comes closer to me. Our lips meet. His kiss is soft and gentle, like it's not a dare but our wedding. No, it's too gentle, even for a wedding.

After a couple more seconds, we break apart. First, our eyes meet, but I quickly avert my gaze. The silence — even lasting for just a second — is too uncomfortable. I wish I was dared to scale a cliff like Blake was. It would've been easier.

"It was nice," says Andy, grinning. It's a stupid thing to say, but it's better than nothing.

Eric's communicator rings. "Hey. What's up?" he says. "Oh, yeah. We're at our spot. See ya."

"Who's that?" asks Blake, holding Avery by the shoulders.

"Black," answers Eric, and I fail to breathe. Not that I care, but I'd better he wouldn't come. I know these are his friends, but come on. His clan is at war, dammit. Doesn't he have better things to do?

"So uh," I stutter. "How long have you all been friends?"

"Years," answers Blake. "We've been through a lot together."

"Yeah," sighs Avery. "But you know, at the end of the day all of us are just adrenaline junkies who have to keep calm at their jobs," she says, smiling. "This friend group is our way of letting things go and just having fun without worrying about the consequences."

I love the sound of this. Might be just what I need.

In what seems like half an hour of conversations and more stupid dares, I hear the roar of an engine. *Bike,* I think. A couple of seconds later, I see I was right. A black, shiny bike emerges from behind the rock at full speed. You must be a complete idiot to ride like that on the mountain road. Or have a death wish.

It comes to us and drifts to a stop. I really can't take my eyes off this masterpiece. I wish I had such a bike.

The rider gets off the bike and now I can't take my eyes off him. Black jeans, leather jacket and gloves, a shiny black helmet that reflects the sun. His moves are sharp and confident. His body is lean and fit. I catch myself literally staring and shake off my daze.

He takes off his helmet, and I suddenly wish he didn't. It's too much. Blue eyes outlined with black eyeliner, cheekbones sharper than knives, skin looks too pale in contrast with coal black hair and clothes. Too fucking stunning. I can't take my eyes off him. It's too good for someone you can't have.

Eric comes to Arthur to greet him. "What's the occasion for make-up?"

"Just had the dress-up-to-the-nines mood," he replies. His ever-arrogant smile appears.

"If I were gay, I wouldn't take my eyes off you," Eric says, and everyone laughs.

Arthur unzips his jacket, uncovering the bandage on his neck.

"What happened?" asks Eric, pointing.

Arthur looks at Sky, grinning, and she rolls her eyes. "We're just trying to find some clean skin on Arthur and getting rid of it," she says.

Arthur snorts. "Come on, I'm not that inked."

"Well, less inked than Blake, who has a whole suit but still," comments Skylar. "Anyway, you have a competitor at getting all tattooed," she adds, pointing at me.

I raise my eyebrows. "Me?"

"You're just 21, and you already have a sleeve and a couple more here and there," Sky says, and I smile.

"I probably should slow down if I don't want to cover myself in a couple of years." I laugh.

Arthur, Eric, Andy, Avery, and Blake stand near the edge of the cliff laughing about something. I join Sky and Alina sitting on the rocks.

"So, you're new to this insane friend group?" I ask Alina, and she nods, smiling slightly. She and Sky look so alike, only Alina is paler. Skylar's skin is such a deep brown and Alina's look like she just spent a little too much time at the beach. Same with their eyes, Sky's are two almost black pools and Alina's are a color of caramel. But it's still easy to see they're sisters.

"And what do you think?" I ask.

"I don't know," she answers. "It's a little too much for me." I guess their biggest differences run on the inside, not the outside.

"I see. I do understand why it can feel overwhelming. It's a little bit for me too, to be honest," I say.

"Really?" she asks, surprised. "It looks like you're here for a thousandth time. Like you belong."

"I may belong," I try to explain, "but it still feels overwhelming. You know, a year ago I was a human and lived with my mom in a village." I stop at that, it's hard to put into words what I feel.

"Thank you for sharing. It's good to feel you're not the only odd one out." Alina smiles.

I'm not sure what she means. I didn't really say anything special, but it seems to help her, anyway. So I nod and smile at her.

"You are more similar than I thought," says Skylar, looking at us. I just raise my eyebrows at her, surprised.

After a pause, Alina says, "I wish I was like you with boys, Lorna." I raise my eyebrows questioningly again. "I mean, I'm almost eighty years old, and I can't get into contact with anyone. Even a kiss is a stress for me, and I can't even imagine what it's like to make love to someone."

"You haven't?" I ask, and she shakes her head. "Do you want to?"

"Maybe if it's someone special," she says, and I smile. It's so cute. And a little funny. I don't judge, of course, but for me, this idea of waiting for the one and only and perceiving sex as something sacred seems a little ridiculous. I never paid it so much attention. But maybe it's a good way to handle it. To wait for this special one to never compare, to think they're the best, to learn together. Sounds sweet.

I hear a burst of laughter and Arthur's voice: "I will remember you this, Blake."

What just happened? I look at them, amused, as they are heading towards us.

"What now?" I say mockingly.

"I just dared him to guess who's who with a kiss," says Blake, smiling broadly. "Sorry," he adds. I stare at him, confused.

"Only the girls," he says. "He closes his eyes, you all kiss him, he guesses. Or doesn't. Easy."

I roll my eyes. "Will there be anyone I'm not kissing today?" I say.

"You only kissed Eric," he protests.

"It's always like that," says Sky to me, rolling her eyes and smiling.

"Idiots" I say. I joke to hide my nervousness. I guess I always do.

"Okay, shall we?" Arthur says indifferently.

"Close your eyes," says Blake. And Arthur does.

Avery points at Sky, so she goes first. She puts her hand on Arthur's shoulder and presses her lips to his. The kiss lasts only for a couple of seconds. Then she pulls back.

Avery is next. She has to stand on her tiptoes to reach him. She wraps her arms around his neck and kisses him like he's her lover she hasn't seen for a couple of months. The kiss is passionate and provocative in some way. As if involuntarily, Arthur puts his hand on her waist. Before breaking the contact, she pulls on his lower lip with her teeth. She returns to Blake's side, and he throws an arm around her, rolling his eyes. She shrugs as if saying, *'it was your idea.'*

I look at Alina, who awkwardly rose from the stone and is heading towards us. She puts her hand on Arthur's waist and kisses him gently. When she pulls away, he frowns a little, as if confused.

It's my turn. I come to him, trying to calm down as I move. *Well, a kiss is not necessarily lips,* I think. So I just kiss him on the cheek. Everyone looks at me, confused, and I shrug, smiling.

"What's your verdict, Black?" asks Blake.

"First Skylar. Third Alina. And second − I hesitated, but the fourth was too obvious. Lorna. Always the rule breaker," Arthur says, looking at me. "Second's logically Avery."

Blake claps his hands a couple of times. "Precise," he says. "Still, I wanna see you kiss," he adds, pointing at Arthur and me. Shit. "That's my new dare."

Arthur grins. "Fine. And I dare you to leave a hickey on Eric's neck."

"What?!" Blake and Eric say together.

"A dare for a dare," Arthur says. "You first," he adds.

Blake comes to Eric and kisses his neck. It looks so awkward I can't not laugh. When he finishes, he wipes his mouth with his palm. "Remind me to never dare you again, Black," he says, and Arthur snorts. "So," Blake says, annoyed, pointing at us.

Arthur turns toward me, and our eyes meet. My heart beats too fast, but I take a step forward, anyway. Arthur puts his hand on the side of my neck and pulls me roughly to him. I unconsciously put my hand on his chest and the other on his waist. His free hand settles on my thigh.

Kissing him is not like kissing Eric. Even though I can see this is just about showing off, he kisses me like I belong to him. Wildly, possessively.

Suddenly, it pisses me off, and I push him away, hard. He takes a step back, looking at me.

"Enough," I say.

Silence hangs in the air. "And what was that?" he asks calmly, arrogantly.

"You know what it's about," I say.

"Tell me." His voice is daring.

I stare at him. At the sides of my vision, I see the bewildered faces of our friends.

"Really?" I ask.

"You started this," he says.

"Um, guys, maybe-" Blake starts, but I put a finger in the air, cutting him off. "Don't," I say. He lifts his hands as if in surrender and takes a step back. For a couple more moments, me and Arthur stare at each other.

"I gotta go," he says and walks to his bike. Without saying anything else, he starts the engine and rides away without even putting on a helmet.

Before he rounds a corner, a car emerges. Arthur breaks and swerves to avoid the accident. Almost at full speed, he crushes into the rock and falls off the bike, rolling on the ground a few times before he stops.

I rush to him, and the guys follow. When I reach Arthur, I see him on the ground unconscious, blood dripping from the wound at his temple. I fall to my knees and press my fingers to his neck. I sigh with relief when I feel a steady beat. I freeze as Eric helps Arthur into the sitting position, his back against the rock.

In a minute, he opens his eyes and looks at us as if in a daze until he regains sight. He gets up, says, "I'm fine," wipes the blood from his face with a hand, and mounts his bike, this time putting on a helmet. I see him disappear around the corner.

I stand in front of everyone, sensing their gazes on my back. Slowly, I turn to them.

"What?" I say as if nothing happened.

"Sorry?" mumbles Blake.

"I think I'll go home," I say and turn to leave, but Alina's voice stops me. "Don't let whatever it was ruin your day. He's not worth it."

Everyone – including me – turns to look at her, confusion on our faces. I didn't think she was capable of saying such things so confidently. There's more than meets the eye, after all. Sometimes the shy and quiet ones are the braver ones in the end.

I smile at her comment. "You're right," I say.

"So, that's how you argue? I didn't think it was that bad," says Eric.

"It wasn't that bad," I say. "Before..." I trail off.

"Before what?" asks Avery. Memories of us flash before my eyes. They stop at Abigail's death and my comment thrown at Arthur.

"It doesn't matter," I say. "We had an argument that made everything worse. That's it. Now let's change the topic."

On the way back, I don't pay attention to anyone and just stare at the distance. Night landscape passes by. It's as dark as I feel inside.

At the castle, I decide to go to Arthur to check on him and talk. I think I may be even ready to apologize. Maybe we can be together again.

I knock on the door. "Open," comes his voice.

I enter and see him near the table with a dismantled shotgun. He once told me that cleaning his weapons calms him down, so that's probably what I'm seeing now. A calming session.

"How are you?" I ask quietly.

"You came here to ask this?" he says, his voice cold.

"I just wanted to know," I shrug.

"It's none of your business," he says, leaving no room for debate, but I find it anyway. "I was worried, that's it," I say.

His jaw tightens. "Get out," he says calmly, but I can sense the irritation in his voice.

"I just wanted to make sure you're okay, and that's how you react?" I say loudly.

A couple of seconds of silence. I hope he reconsiders.

"Like you care at least a little!" he shouts, slamming his hand on the table. "About anything connected to me!"

Sadness, despair, and anger boil inside me. My expression turns cold. "I am not a stone," I say. "I can't just *not* care. You are so broken you don't feel anything. And you probably think I am as broken as you are. But I'm not. I'm not that weak. So I feel things, even for a jerk like you. My heart is breakable, you know. And maybe it is broken, but it doesn't mean I don't feel anything. I am not you. I am not *like* you." I leave immediately when I finish my outburst of emotions and slam the door.

I go down the stairs, outside, and towards the lake. I almost run.

When I'm at the shore, I scream into the darkness of the waters. I desperately want to punch something, but there's nothing around. So I dig my nails into my arm, trying to bury my mental pain in physical. It helps, but not much. I doubt anything in the world can heal such wounds.

In about an hour, I'm calm again with a couple of new songs written.

"It's over. He's the past," I tell myself one last time, take a deep breath of the cool night air and head back. When I get to my room, I'm so mentally exhausted that I fall asleep at once.

The next day, I meet with Ruby. She has just broken up with her boyfriend I didn't even know she had. Apparently, they met while she was serving in her first division, and then he transferred with her to another one.

Her best friend died, and then her boyfriend left her. I wouldn't wish that on my worst enemy. But she still smiled — genuinely — when she saw me earlier today. She still laughed at my jokes, and she's still the same old Ruby. Cheerful and sweet, despite everything that happened to her.

I look at her sitting in front of me at her kitchen table and tears well up in my eyes. But these tears aren't for her story, they are for her bravery. These are the tears of hope that we can still be alright. We might be at war now, but I see our victory right in front of me. The people who can smile after every heartbreak life throws at them can never be defeated.

We've been talking about her ex for quite some time now. I don't think I am a good advisor when it comes to relationships, but she probably just needs a shoulder to cry on. Well, that I can be.

"You know, it was nice, but I don't care that we broke up," she states with fake confidence. "He was an idiot. I've already forgotten him. It doesn't hurt." I know she's just reassuring herself.

I sit here, closely listening to what Ruby says, but I don't seem to hear anymore. Deleting everything that ever connected you to someone you lost just to forget them so it will hurt less... Well, maybe it works for some people. But I don't believe that denying your feelings helps you to let go. I choose another way. I cry my eyes out when no one sees. I write songs that will break many hearts. I replay our best moments in my head just to remind myself that it's in the past. I let myself feel and, therefore move on.

CHAPTER 36

NUMB

When I've healed, I immediately went to my post. I loved working with my latest division, and my captain – Levi – approved of me, too. She said I was really invested and she could count on me to make fast decisions. That I can definitely do.

I get out of the truck and see Levi's smiling face. Her long blond curls fall on her shoulders, which tells me she was getting ready to sleep before I arrived. She never walks around without her hair in a bun.

"Hey, how are things?" I say in greeting.

"Boring without you." She grins. I hug her.

"You must be tired from your trip here. Go rest," she says warmly. "I have a few tasks for you for tomorrow."

I nod. I love that she already knows she can throw me into missions at once. I go to my tent to have some sleep before tomorrow.

Days and weeks blur together in my mind once again. I guess that's how life is on the frontline. Wake up, get a task, do the task, go to bed. Once in a while I get some free time and train if I'm lucky.

The sounds of war don't scare me anymore. But the war itself scares me more and more each day. It just shouldn't exist.

What are we even fighting for? That thought crosses my mind from time to time.

These missions, these battles – they don't make sense. The forest, the lab, the damned cave during the training. None of these make sense.

I'm starting to feel that we're fighting a war we know nothing about. And I fear I might be fighting for the wrong things. I'm not questioning my loyalty to Arthur, even if we aren't together anymore. I know him well enough to trust that he would never fight for any wrong ideals. But what if he doesn't see the whole picture, either?

Is it even possible to see the whole picture while at war? Furthermore, Arthur never really talked much about the war or the reasoning behind it. And for whatever reason, I never asked about it either. He said that they were at war with Vivian's clan before, but I never asked him for details. Did he mean the Great War – the one after which the lands were divided?

We were attacked, I get as much. And we have to protect ourselves and our territories, that I get as well. But I have no idea why we were attacked in the first place or what happened between our clans before.

I guess I should have asked for more details after all. It scares me that I might be fighting for the wrong cause just because I don't know everything.

But for now, another day, another battle.

A soldier fires her gun, and a bullet hits my arm. I don't care much and continue fighting. Not the first time and definitely not the last.

In a few minutes, though, I start feeling like I don't have an arm. It shouldn't be like that. I feel a little dizzy. And then it hits me.

The bullet was poisoned. I need to retreat so I don't get killed. I take a few steps back, dodging a blow from my opponent, and then my legs refuse me, and I fall to the ground. My whole body paralyzed.

I try to move, but it's no use. I don't feel my body at all. It's like it doesn't belong to me.

In my peripheral vision, I see two soldiers coming to me. They lift me by the arms and drag me somewhere. All I can see is the ground and my own feet that I don't feel.

I hear a car door open, and the soldiers throw me inside. Then the car drives away.

I put all my will into it and try to move, but I can't even lift a finger. After a few more attempts, I black out.

I wake up in a cell. As I realize that, a wave of panic surges through me. *What now?* I get up on my elbows and look around. The place is dark and damp.

I get up and come closer to the bars to get a better look. When I touch them, I feel sharp pain. Electricity. Fuck, I should've thought of this. I keep looking around anxiously, not knowing what to do. Can I really do anything?

I sit on the floor at the back of the cell and try to calm down.

In what seems like too long – though I know it's not – a soldier comes and opens my cell door. I get up and try to fight, but I'm too weak, so she manages to drag me out. She drags me into some other room, where she handcuffs me to a wall.

"So, let's talk," she says. "I only need to know your clan's plans. That's all. Tell me, and I won't make you suffer." She grins.

I'm afraid of what she might do, but I can't tell her anything. I just keep silent.

"I asked a question," she says. I keep silent, my eyes on the floor.

I realize it doesn't look too good, and I lift my head to face her. I look into her eyes defiantly. Fake confidence, my old friend.

"Okay," she says and hits my face. I moan slightly, my cheek hurts.

"Tell me now?" I keep silent, and for some reason, I grin.

For some time she keeps hitting me, only stopping to ask if I'm ready to tell her. But I do not relent. I won't betray my clan. Definitely not because of a few bruises.

When she's done with me, she drags my limp body back to the cell and says, before leaving, "See you tomorrow."

I don't want another day of this. Please…

I would cry if I was sure no one was watching me.

CHAPTER 37

SHELTER

I was so beat up yesterday that most of my bruises haven't even managed to heal. But obviously, no one cares, so I'm cuffed to the wall again.

The same woman asks if I'm ready to give up and betray my clan – she uses different words, of course, but it doesn't matter – but my answer stays the same. It will always stay the same.

She hits me in the stomach with her foot and then in the head with her hand. I get dizzy for a few seconds, but it's fine.

She looks at me and narrows her eyes in thought. Then she takes a knife out of the sheath of her pants and says, "Time to make things more fun, don't you think?" *No, I fucking don't.* I stay silent.

She stabs my thigh, and I cry out, not expecting her to start this dramatically. I dare to look down and see the knife stick out of me. Nice.

She grabs it and takes it out of me, and I see blood stain my pants immediately. That can't be good.

The woman cuts my arm open, blood gashes out of the wound, and drips from my arm to the grey concrete floor. She brings her knife to her lips and licks the blade. *Gross.*

I meet her eyes, and we stare at each other for a few moments. Then she cuts my tank top – I usually wear it under my armor – open. She traces my already bruised stomach with the knife, occasionally making deeper cuts. She does the same to my chest and arms, and after just a little time, my whole body hurts.

She keeps hitting and cutting me and I lose track of time. All I can concentrate on is keeping my mouth shut. I feel like I'm breaking. Just some more effort, and I might tell them. I'm not strong enough.

Then I hear a voice inside my head. Arthur's voice: *'You're stronger than me. I know you don't believe it, but it's true. I can never be like you.'*

I remember when he told me this. We were sitting on the floor of his balcony at night. I remember how cold I was. Arthur dragged a blanket outside and covered us with it. I asked if he was cold too, but he said he just wanted to be close to me so he would have to soldier through being covered with a blanket, even though he was rather warm.

He encased me in his arms, and I just started crying for no reason. I mean, I had a reason, I was just so happy to have him next to me and so afraid of losing him. I told him exactly that.

"You're so comfortable with your emotions," he said.

"Only when I'm with you," I countered.

"Still, it comes naturally to you. I mean, you even dared to say you loved me first." He laughed.

"Well, maybe there's some truth to it," I agreed as my tears dried.

"I mean it, Rebel, you're stronger than me. I know you don't believe it, but it's true. I can never be like you. I can never let my emotions flow that easily. Not even with you. Please, don't get me wrong, I love you and I trust you, but I just can't. It's too hard. It's scary."

Suddenly, I realize I almost don't feel anything in the real world. I can make a shelter in my mind. I can escape reality.

I remember more moments. Moments that I hold dear to my heart. How Arthur kissed me for the first time, how he told me he was proud of me, how he told me he thought I was brave. And it works. I don't feel anything. I can pull through.

CHAPTER 38

SAVIOR

The woman drags me to the torture room for what feels like a thousandth time. Maybe it is. I don't care much anymore. As she cuffs me to the wall, I go to the safe place I've created in my head. I see the faces of my friends, remember the things we did together. I feel warmth spreading through my body, not letting pain in. I close my eyes. They can do whatever they want, they can't break me.

I remember how I met my friends, the moment when I realized Roy was my brother, our girls' nights. I even feel my lips form the smallest of smiles.

I throw a glance at the clock. I've been here for more than an hour, so longer than usual. She used to torture me for about 40 minutes at most. I can barely stick to my mind shelter already. But she doesn't seem to be about to stop.

I feel my body start trembling. Everything hurts. My vision blurs and slowly darkens as if I'm sleepy.

This goes on for even more time. Half an hour maybe, I'm not sure. I can't exactly see the clock anymore.

When she's done for the day and she drags me through the hallways, I don't feel much. I think I'm on a new level of shutting down. A level of 'I don't care.'

She literally throws me inside the cell. I feel like I'm dying, my body limp. The woman delivers one final blow to my head with her leg and leaves, slamming the gate shut. My body aches, the ringing in my ears too loud to ignore. I try to get up, but my body refuses me. I'm unable to move at all.

After a couple of long minutes, I start feeling sleepy. Obviously, I don't want to sleep right now, but that's just how I would describe the feeling. I feel like I'm falling into the abyss, into nothingness. I try to resist it, but soon I can't, so I just surrender to it, though I don't want to. As I fall further into the black, I feel proud of myself. They broke my body, but not my mind.

Darkness. Sounds. Voices. I'm being moved.

Everything feels like I'm sleeping, but it's not deep. I open my eyes a little. Someone is carrying me in their arms. I focus a little better and realize it's a man. Black armor, dark hair, hands either just dirty or inked.

Through half-consciousness, I ask, "Where are you carrying me?" Or at least that's what I want to say, but my voice is too weak. No answer follows. I try to force my eyes open and my mind fully awake, but I fail.

In a couple of minutes, the man puts me down and into a sitting position against the wall.

"Lorna," he whispers, touching my shoulder. His voice seems familiar, but I can't quite place it. I try to focus to make out who's in front of me. It seems to me I literally stare at him like a person with a bad sight stares at everything when they forget their glasses. However, I know I don't look like that, I'm too weak to show such effort.

"Lorna, are you there?" the voice asks, more commanding this time.

"I'm... what... yeah..." I murmur. I don't quite understand the message behind my own statement, but that's all I can manage.

"Don't move and be silent," the man says quickly, warning in his voice, and then he goes somewhere. I hear something. Gunshots? Or maybe that's just the ringing in my ears.

A couple more bangs, and the sound dies down as the man returns to me. I want to ask for his name, but I don't have enough time before he takes me into his arms again.

Some time of running long hallways, and he puts me in the front seat of a car. Do I have to drive? I laugh at my own thought. Of course not, it's nonsense. I can't even walk.

The man sits next to me in the driver's seat and starts the engine, and the car starts moving. I feel like I'm about to lose consciousness again. I try to fight it, this time harder. But soon I disconnect from reality, anyway.

I'm in the kitchen, cooking. From time to time, I check the clock. Soon the front door opens and two kids run into the room.

"Hey Mommy," says the girl and hugs me. In a couple of seconds, the boy joins her. Just when they let go of me, Brad enters. His light brown hair clings to his sweaty forehead and his green eyes are bright with joy. I smile as I remember how we used to sneak out of our houses at night to meet when we were at school. I can't believe now he's my husband, and we have two children.

After having dinner together, Brad helps me clean up, and then we go to put the kids to bed. We kiss them goodnight and leave their room.

"Honey," I say, "I love you."

"I love you too," he answers warmly.

I bite my lip because *'I love you'* is not what I wanted to say. Actually, it was that I'm somehow worried, anxious. I don't know why, there's no real reason for that. So all in all, I decided not to share with Brad.

It's just nonsense. I'm just paranoid.

I stand in front of the mirror and look at myself. Blond hair falls on my shoulders and covers them. Grey eyes, pale skin. I wear a plain dress and simple shoes. A girl should be modest.

For a while, I stare at myself, and then the reflection starts changing. My hair darkens and becomes dark blue. Facial features turn sharper, and the look in my eyes turns from soft and loving to dangerous and powerful. A scar cuts across my left eye.

No, it's not me, I think as a chill runs down my spine. Though she looks like me just... after some awful events. The woman in front of me wears a black T-shirt, and her arms and collarbones are covered with ink. For a few minutes, she stays in the mirror looking at me and then disappears, and I appear again.

Suddenly, I smell smoke. What's going on? I run to the hallway and see the smoke coming from the children's bedroom. No...

I open the door and see the room on fire. With my feet glued to the floor, I start screaming. In a couple of seconds, Brad comes and rushes into the room.

"Lorna, get out!" he shouts.

I run out of the house and wait for them outside. And then the house explodes.

I stand in front of my house – no, of what's left of it – as burning parts of wood fall around me.

"No," I whisper. How could it happen? How could it happen? *How could it happen?!*

I want to run to the wreckage to look for my family, though I know I can't do anything. I want to scream for help, though I know no one can help me. I feel helpless. I just stand there, voiceless, paralyzed. I can't do anything. *I can't do anything.* I'm just a woman. A housewife. Practically no one.

Help! Anyone! I scream in my head, but of course no one hears me.

I jerk awake and realize I was dreaming. What the hell? Why would I dream about my school ex-boyfriend, us having kids, me being some... some... '*right*' woman? That's fucking crazy.

I feel a little better now. At least I can see straight. I stare out of the window and see trees pass by. Where are we going? Who is my savior? Did he even want to save me, or was it something else? I think I can just ask. But will he answer? If he does, will it be an honest answer? Can I even speak legibly?

Fuck!

I've never doubted myself so much. Probably the realization that you can't help yourself if need be does make a person insecure. But *I'm not someone who can't help herself*, I remind myself.

I close my eyes and turn my head towards the ceiling, and without opening them, ask, "Where-" I realize the word doesn't really leave my throat. I'm still too weak. I gather all my strength. "Where are we going?" I ask finally.

At first, no answer follows, and I start thinking he didn't actually hear my question. I want to repeat it, but he says, "Safe place."

Safe place? What does that even mean? "Who are-" *you* I want to add but stop, realizing. I open my eyes and turn my head towards the driver. "What the hell is going on?" I demand, unexpectedly harsh, even for myself.

Turning on his usual smirk, Arthur says, "That's your version of a 'thank you'?"

"Why should I-" I start, but remember, he actually just saved my life. "Thank you," I say. "But the question still waits for its answer."

"I'll tell you later, when we're safe. Better get some sleep. It was easier for me to drive while you were unconscious."

At first, I want to snap back, but why the fuck do I even care? I turn back to the window and tears well up in my eyes. *Do you really not know how much I want you to hold me right now?*

I decide it's actually better to drift off, so I close my eyes, and remembering how his arms were once my safety, I fall asleep.

I wake up in bed covered with a warm blanket. The room is plain, with not much furniture, all in light colors. It looks like a usual house, though I'm sure it's not. No windows, I note.

I feel too weak to move or to even think, so I decide my best option is to sleep and try to recover. If I'm with Arthur, I'm safe.

For some time, I just get in and out of consciousness. Arthur comes to check on me every once in a while. A couple of times I even tried to stand up, but quickly gave up on this idea.

In a while, I can stay awake when I want to. It's already something. Still, I won't dare to stand up yet. Arthur brought me some water and blood to drink so I could get better faster. Turns out the woman broke my body more than I realized.

When I finally find strength in myself to get up, I go to take a shower. Bloody water goes down the drain, and I feel little stings from the places where it touches my still healing wounds. So practically everywhere.

I walk out of the bathroom completely naked because my clothes and even underwear are soaked with blood. And as for now, I have neither strength nor desire to wash them.

There's a wardrobe in the room, so maybe there's some spare clothes there. I go to check, and there actually is. A couple of T-shirts and pairs of pants, even a few pairs of underwear. Arthur probably thought it all through in case a group of people had to use the place for a while. What is this place, by the way? I find some boxers that kind of fit me, pants, and a T-shirt. After putting it all on, I decide to get out of the room.

I open my door and see two other doors, one on each side of the hallway. At the end of it, is the staircase.

I almost crawl down the stairs – every single step feels odd – and see Arthur sleeping on a couch. I come closer to it and throw a glance at him. My lips turn into a small smile, and my eyes become watery.

"How could we let it go so easily?" I whisper and bite my lip. I suddenly feel a strong urge to snuggle close to him. To remember for at least one more time that I'm still afraid of everything that's going on and of what's coming. To one more time remind myself that I'm still alive, that I still feel, that I still can let myself be vulnerable.

I realize it's a bad idea considering everything between us and the last time I tried to make peace, but I can't help myself. I come closer and sit on the couch next to him. I look at his face and take the sheet he's covered with and then lie down, turning my back to him. It's not as close as I would love to be, but it will do. If later he has questions as to why I decided to lie with him, I can say I'm still afraid of darkness – which is true – and I feel better around someone. He's not a monster after all, he will understand. And if anything, the bed upstairs is a bloody mess, so I wouldn't want to sleep in it, anyway.

For a while, I lie with my eyes open, thinking. What was that dream about? Was it what my life would've been if I'd decided to go the way my mother wanted me to? Would I really be so helpless and indecisive? Of course, I couldn't stand a chance against fire and an explosion. But I didn't even *try*.

I didn't even try. The thought scares me more than anything else. How could I not? Is that what it means to be a 'right' woman? To cry for help? To stand by when everything around you is falling apart? When the ones you love die? Or is it to be so forced into 'right,' into having a family that you just do what you're told without any feelings, so then one day you discover you just don't care what happens to your family?

No, I did care, I interrupt my train of thought. I know that. I was there, I felt that. I cared. Just didn't dare to do anything. Is that what I was supposed to be?

I close my eyes when I feel Arthur move. Pretending I'm sleeping... well, really amazing behavior for an adult woman who is, moreover, a soldier on the frontline. I guess we all go a little childish sometimes.

"Lorna," he whispers, but I don't answer and keep playing my role. I almost jump from surprise when he kisses my temple and wraps his arm around me. Driven by an impulse and the thought that I might be not the only one who misses us, I dare to turn and snuggle closer to him. He wraps his arm tighter around me like he used to do every time I was down.

"You're safe now, it's okay," he whispers. I don't say anything and just let all the tears I was holding out. Maybe I'll regret it later, but now I don't care, I still trust him. After some time, I drift off.

In what seems like a couple of hours, I wake up still in Arthur's arms. I turn to lie on my back and stare at the ceiling.

"How are you feeling?" Arthur asks.

"Better," I say unemotionally, like nothing happened. Like I didn't just cry on his shoulder.

After a couple of silent seconds, he rises on his elbow and kisses me, first on my forehead and then the lips. The kiss is so soft, gentle, and somehow caring.

"I thought I lost you," he says quietly, as if afraid to say it out loud.

I can't find anything to tell him, so I just stare at him, knowing how stupid it must look. And then I can't stand the distance between us, so I press my lips to his, and he answers immediately.

I put my hands under his T-shirt and feel his skin under my fingers. I start pulling the T-shirt off him, and when we have to break away from each other, he puts his hand in front of him as if asking me to stop. "Lorna, you're not in the state for that."

"I'm fine," I say, even though I know I'm not. My body is so broken that probably his every touch will cause pain, but now I don't care. I need him. Now. I need to know he's still mine.

He kisses me again and says, "No, you're not. We'll have time for that, now you need to heal."

"Please," I almost beg him. "Please, I need you."

"I don't think you're thinking straight," he says and lies down next to me.

"Art, I'm absolutely sane and sober, what else do you need? It's my body that's not alright, not my mind," I say, smiling because even though I don't like his idea of stopping, I appreciate his care for me. Yeah, the exact protective care because of which we broke up. I feel stupid. I can't even decide if I like it or not.

"I can decide for myself," I add, but I still see doubt in his eyes. "Don't be afraid to hurt me. You won't."

After a couple of seconds, he finally gives up, takes off his T-shirt and kisses me. He pulls off the T-shirt I'm wearing, and I feel the warmth of his body against mine.

For a while, he looks at my body, not like he usually did, but as if assessing the damage. Then first, he kisses my lips again, then my neck, then the chest, then going lower and lower until he reaches my hip line. My body aches from his touch, but the pain feels pleasant because he's all I want now. He keeps kissing me as he pulls my pants and boxers down my legs, and the moment I feel his tongue on me is the moment I actually stop thinking straight.

I dig my fingers into his hair and writhe beneath his touch. Arthur lifts my legs and puts them on his shoulders, then stops and looks up at me from between my legs. *Damn.*

He puts his hands on my hips, squeezing lightly, and I let out a whimper.

"Sorry," he murmurs against my skin and goes back to devouring me.

"Art," I gasp and grind against his mouth. I feel him smile.

He steadily drives me to an orgasm, and when I fall over the edge, I can't hold back anymore and start chanting his name. It feels so good even though my whole body aches. I want to fucking die with his name on my tongue.

"Enough for you," Art says and smiles. I smile back.

He kisses me, and I taste my own arousal on his lips. I wrap my arms around him, probably tighter than I should.

"Get some rest," he says, kissing my forehead. He lies next to me, and I rest my head on his chest, his arms wrapped around me. I'm finally back home.

CHAPTER 39

ECHOES OF THE PAST

I open my eyes and stretch. We've been staying at Arthur's bunker house – yes, he has a bunker house – for about a week already. I feel better each day, soon I'll be back in the fight.

I see Arthur at the table, lost in thought. I throw on his T-shirt, get up, and walk to him.

"What are you doing?" I ask.

"I need to plan our next moves," he says. "I mean, not *ours*," he gestures between me and him. "The clan."

I nod. "Can I help?"

"Sure," he says.

I pull a chair and sit next to him.

"I want to target their key positions, get as close as we can to the heart, if you will. I want to know for sure who's behind all this," Arthur says, half to me and half to himself.

"Behind this?" I echo.

"Vivian is rather young. I'm sure she has..." he pauses for the briefest second. "Allies."

"Do you know who they might be?"

"Unfortunately, I do," Arthur says. "During the Great War, Vivian's clan was allied with two others. One of them was destroyed, and their leader – Ivy Levynn – was killed. Most of her people either died with her or fled. And the other one..." he trails off, his eyes darken. "The other one was a pain in my ass for quite some time now. Marius Renard was the one who killed my parents."

"Do you think he might be the one helping Vivian?" I ask quietly.

"I just don't see who else would. But Marius is smart, and Vivian keeps making stupid mistakes. I don't think we see the whole picture," he says, and I can almost see the gears shifting in his head.

I've been thinking as much. We don't see the whole picture, and I hate it.

"So, targeting key positions, you said?"

"Yeah," he starts, but I interrupt him, "Wait."

Harley once told me that there's an agreement to fight only army against army. Maybe we can at least ask for that?

"Do you think Vivian would agree to fight army to army? Somewhere on a neutral ground," I suggest.

"That's what I thought of, too. I even wanted to ask for a one-on-one battle to finish all that. One battle to the death."

"Like two soldiers?" I ask.

"Yeah. I know she'd never agree, though," Arthur answers. "Even if it wasn't her who fought. She's a trained fighter, but she wouldn't risk herself," he says, disgust evident in his voice.

"Who would you put? If she agreed."

"Myself. That's the only option," he states.

"You're so confident you'd win?"

"Honestly, yes. But also I wouldn't allow it to be anyone else," he explains, and I nod. I'd do the same. "Anyway, army against army it is. I think we can try to negotiate that. What do you think about the place?" he asks.

I mentally list all the possible options and then say, "The valley next to the train station, right where the mountains start. We'll have a higher ground."

"There's a village there. We'll be fighting right near civilians," he counters.

"Near *houses*," I correct. "Everyone there is either dead or has long fled."

It sounds terrible, but... after some thinking, I would give up my house to have a home to return to.

"I heard you," he says tensely. "You're good at that," he adds.

"I only say what I think. That's not difficult." I smile.

"Well, yes, but most people also don't do that." He gets up and embraces and kisses me.

"Listen, I know we didn't part on good terms and-" Arthur starts, but before he can go on, I put my finger to his lips, silencing him.

We lock eyes for a few seconds, and then we kiss. We definitely have problems that we will have to address in the future, but at this moment I don't care.

Art lifts me and sits me on the table, papers with his plans fall to the floor. His hands roam under my T-shirt, his lips devour mine with inhumane hunger.

As he stops, he says, "Drink me," and tilts his head to expose his neck to me.

I put my hand on one side of his neck and bite into the tender skin. Blood fills my mouth, and I moan from the overwhelming pleasure of his taste. I drink until I know I have to stop, but it doesn't feel nearly enough. I want all of him. I want to fucking bleed him dry.

I kiss him, and he whispers a shaky "I love you" into my lips.

"I love you too. So much," I return.

I wrap my arms around him and drink in his smell, his warmth, his everything. "Please, don't ever let me go again," I whisper.

"I won't," he promises.

I take off his sweatshirt and run my hands over his chest and abs. Not wanting to wait any longer, I take off my T-shirt as well.

Arthur puts his hand on my neck, squeezing, and flicks his tongue over my nipple before biting it lightly. I whimper as my body twitches, and he squeezes my neck harder, just enough to make breathing difficult. I claw at his hand, but he only smiles against my skin.

"I can't breathe," I choke out.

"That's the point," he says arrogantly.

"Asshole," I manage. He lets go of my throat, but only to slap me on the cheek.

"Ouch," I say playfully.

"Ouch will be when I make your ass red," he says. "In fact, I remember making this threat once already. Time to go through with it, don't you think?"

Before I can respond, he takes me off the table and turns me around, my back now pressed to his front.

"Bend," he whispers in my ear, but I ignore it.

He slides my boxers down my legs and slaps my ass. "Ouch," I repeat.

"Not yet," he says as he pushes me to lay my upper body on the table.

I hear the sound of a zipper, and in just a moment, he enters me. I gasp and push myself away from the table, but he slams me back with the hand on the back of my neck. His other hand connects with my ass.

"Ouch?" I say and can't help but laugh.

"You're insufferable, you know that?" Arthur asks, and I hear the smile in his voice.

I giggle, but he shuts me up with another slap. He puts his hands on my hips and thrusts into me, occasionally planting yet another slap to my ass.

I grip the table and moan his name when he hits just the right spot inside me. My ass burns, but it makes everything even better.

"Not so talkative now, are we?" Arthur says in my ear before tracing with his tongue up my neck. Then he grips my hair in his hand and pulls, lifting my head off the table. He slaps my ass again.

"It hurts," I say.

"Oh, it better do," he answers and does it yet again.

He brings his fingers to my clit and circles it until I come all over him. He follows right after and turns me to face him. He puts his fingers into my mouth and I lick them.

"Mine," he says.

"Yours," I agree.

CHAPTER 40

ETERNALLY YOURS

After a few more days of half strategizing, half fucking, we decide it's time to go back to the castle to actually execute our plans. Our little getaway vacation's been going on for too long already.

The ride home is surprisingly uneventful. At the gate, a few soldiers meet us. The first thing I do is ask if my friends are here. It's not that I want to talk to them right now, but I'm pretty sure they are worried, so I guess I should let them know I'm alive. Roy turns out to be the only one home, and I'm grateful for that.

"I'll go see Roy," I tell Arthur as we get out of the car.

"Sure," he answers. "Will you come to me for the night?" he asks, and I nod, smiling.

I go to Roy's room and knock on his door.

"Open."

I carefully peek inside. "Hey," I say.

"Lorna!" he exclaims, and in a second he's suffocating me with his embrace. "I'm so happy you're alive."

"Not for long if you keep doing that to me," I manage to choke out.

"Sorry." He chuckles. "Where the hell have you been?" Concern fills his eyes as he asks that.

"Well, it's a long story."

I tell him about my time as a captive and briefly about staying at the bunker house with Arthur.

"I knew he'd save you," Roy says. "He was worried sick. It showed in a way he got angry literally over anything."

"Isn't that Arthur's usual state?" I ask, smiling.

"Not to *that* extent. You should've seen it."

His words fill me with some unexplainable warmth. Arthur was worried about me even after my freaking out about Abigail, even despite him saying he didn't want to see me again.

My thoughts are interrupted by a knock. Roy stands up from the bed to open the door. Randy steps into the room and immediately catches Roy with a kiss. At first, I stare at them, surprised, and then turn away, realizing that I'm witnessing something rather private.

When they break away from each other, Randy notices me. "Oh, hey," he says.

I wave at him, smiling awkwardly.

"I didn't know you were here," he says. "You ok? Heard you had some pretty rough adventures."

"All good," I say. "Well, I'll leave you two then." I wink at Roy and leave his room. I need to do something before I go to Arthur.

I never gave myself to him. I wanted to, but we broke up, and I didn't really have time. So I'm doing it today. Waiting doesn't usually end well. Especially at war.

I enter his room and find him sitting at the table, papers all over it.

"More planning?" I ask.

"Mhm," he murmurs without even turning to me, clearly lost in thought.

I come to him and put my hands on his bare shoulders, massaging lightly. He groans quietly and tilts his head back at my touch.

"I need to finish this," he sighs, as if it's difficult for him to refuse me. It would definitely be difficult for *me* if our positions were reversed.

I decide to let him finish whatever he's doing and go sit on the couch to wait for him. In some time, he joins me.

"Hey," he says and kisses me. I smile against him and wrap my arms around his neck.

"I have something for you," I say and bite my lip nervously. I'd better do it now before I chicken out completely and not do it at all. I mean, I know he loves me, but it's still scary.

I give him the pendant filled with my blood, my name engraved on the crystal.

He takes it from my hand, and his eyes meet mine. I'm not sure, but I think I see tears glistening in them. He kisses me and hugs me before I even manage to say anything.

"I'm eternally yours," I half whisper. "I love you."

He pulls back to look at me, and I was right about the tears after all.

"I can't express how happy I am," he says, wiping a tear from his cheek.

I wrap my arms around his neck. "Were you expecting something different?" I ask.

"You just didn't say anything about this, you never wore my crystal. I..." he stumbles. "I don't know. I was more than ready for the possibility that you don't want this. Don't want *me*."

"Idiot," I say. "You know I love you, and you know I like this tradition. I never wore yours, but I always had it with me. I just wanted us to put them on together, but we broke up and all, you know."

I hand him the crystal he's given me. "Will you?" I point at my neck as I turn and take my hair out of the way. He lays the necklace on me and secures the lock. I do the same for him. We seal our deal with a kiss.

CHAPTER 41

LAST WORDS

After some time of back and forth with Vivian's soldiers – since she never agreed to meet with Arthur herself – we finally have an agreement. One final battle to decide it all. Away from civilians, just army against army.

It's going to be a bloodbath. I'm not looking forward to that part. And honestly, I'm rather doubtful of that whole plan, even though I kind of suggested it myself.

Okay, let's say we win the battle, and then what? Does anyone actually believe Vivian will stop at that? Because I don't. She refused to even sign any agreement, and it's fair to say I don't believe her word alone. I'm not even sure I'd believe a signed agreement.

But anyway, I take my weapons and my armor and whatever's left of my focus and sanity and leave my room.

We get to the battlefield camp. We have less than 24 hours until it all starts. I need to get as much rest as I can, so I lie down to try to fall asleep.

When I wake after a restless sleep a few hours later, I get dressed and just stand in the middle of the tent, trying to collect myself. I'm extremely nervous and I don't know why. Is it because I know the battle will be bloody? Or because I'm scared of losses that will surely follow? Or is it because I get that familiar feeling that all of this is wrong? This isn't a final battle. I want to believe it is, but I don't.

I hear someone enter my tent and turn to face Arthur. Already ready and dressed in his armor.

"So, let's do this," I say as I look at him.

"Maybe you should stay behind," he offers.

"What?" I ask, confused.

"It will get bloody out there. I want you to be safe."

I open and close my mouth a few times like a fish. Completely at a loss for words.

"What?" I repeat. I feel tears at the back of my eyes. He can't be serious.

"Look, I know you want a part in it. And I know that you're more than capable of not only defending yourself but also fighting. But it will get way worse than what you've been through already. I'd rather you do not directly engage."

"You can't be serious," I say, my voice weak. "You know I'm a good fighter. I trained for that. You said I was the best." I raise my voice as strength returns to it.

"Lorna, I don't mean-"

"Enough," I cut him off. "Just enough. Why do you always do this? Do you never learn?"

"Lorna," he pleads.

"No," I spat. "Leave it. Just... just leave me alone." My voice shakes.

"Please." Arthur takes a step toward me and reaches for my hand.

I take a step back. "Damn your overprotectiveness. I hate it," I pause.

"I hate you," I say and run out of the tent as tears fall from my eyes. Why is it always like that? Why can't he just not care about me for a damn minute?

I go to join my division. Fuck Arthur and what he thinks. Like it ever mattered if he approved.

I push him out of my head for now – or maybe forever – I have more important things to focus on.

I take a detour and climb up a hill near what will be the battlefield too soon for my liking. At the top, I approach Blake and Avery, who are stationed there. "How are things?" I ask.

Blake points to where Vivian's army is. "They're ready," he says grimly.

"So are we," I answer confidently.

But I look down at the field in horror. This is where it will end. This is where our two armies will dance. At least the civilians are out of range. *That* if we win. If we don't...

I don't want to think about that possibility, but I let the thought into my mind, anyway. If we don't win, Vivian will destroy everything we hold dear. She will torture and kill. She will stop at nothing to turn everything into a wasteland that only bows to her. With that in mind, I come down, letting the anger and fear for our people fuel my determination.

I join my division where our people and Vivian's stand in front each other. Army to army.

To my right, there's a mountain with a see-through cave at the very top. As soon as the sun shines through it, the battle will begin. Vampire dramatics. For whatever reason, it makes me smile and my eyes start to burn.

The moment later, I feel warmth on my skin and see the field illuminated with the light. And the commotion begins.

We rush at each other swinging and shooting, and at first, it starts okay. I fight effortlessly and feel like we can actually win.

I still use the sword Arthur gave me as my birthday gift. I lost it the day I was captured, but thankfully it was left right where it fell from my hand, and my captain recovered it.

I get deeper into enemy lines, and the battle starts feeling more and more fierce.

Each time I kill someone, I leave a scar on myself. One can say I got used to it, but damn, you can't get used to that if you care at least a little. These people might be terrible, but there are someones out there who loved them. It probably shouldn't hurt, but it does. It hurts to think that a son might not see his mother because I killed her. It shouldn't be that way. I hope that someday there will be no bloodshed, no wars. But not now... Now I have to protect *my* loved ones. It's kill or be killed. I'm sorry, but I don't see any other way.

I approach a wounded soldier. "Surrender," I say. *Please. I don't want to kill you.*

He lifts his gun, and before I can do anything, he shoots himself in the head. I let myself stand there shocked for a few moments, before I'm sucked back into the fight.

A few more soldiers kill themselves right before my eyes, and I can't help but wonder why. We aren't going to kill prisoners. In fact, we will return them safely home if we win. *When* we win. But maybe that's the point? Maybe they don't want to return? Maybe they know that if they do, they will be thrown into Vivian's killing machine yet again. It's all so fucked up.

For the next few hours, I kill and kill, my mind numb, my movements automatic. I fight until all I see around me are bodies and retreating Vivian's soldiers.

CHAPTER 42

IT CAN'T BE

I feel blood running down my face. Blood on my hands and armor, on my sword. I wipe it off my leg.

I look around, seeing bodies on the ground and blood flooding the field. Birds – probably crows and vultures – circle overhead, ready to feast. A chill runs down my spine.

I walk along the line of houses – or what used to be houses – checking the alleys for enemies.

I hear a muffled shout coming from the burned building, not too far to my left. I rush there, maybe someone needs help.

As I near the place, I see Arthur going inside. It fills me with relief to know he's alive. We've lost a lot today, but knowing that he's fine makes up for it for me. It doesn't matter that we argued. I care about him deeply. I know he's not mine anymore, but we've been through it already. Maybe we can make it right again.

I get closer to the building anyway, and as I near it, it explodes.

I'm thrown away by the force of the blow. I open my eyes and look at the burning remains, the pieces of burned tissue drift on the wind around me.

"No!" a scream escapes me, my voice doesn't sound like mine. I try to get up, but my body fails me. But it's not an option, so eventually I get up, anyway. Limping and falling after each couple of steps, I get closer to the building... to the place where it was.

I fall to my knees when I see it up close. When all I see is a complete mess. Pieces of what used to be the building and raging fire. "No," I whisper. I want to scream and cry, but not a single tear comes out. I'm numb. Completely numb.

I sit there, just staring at the flames as the fire burns my skin. I can't move, can't say anything, can't breathe.

In a couple of minutes, shock subsides, and I start crying. I cover my face with my hands. *This can't be. This just can't be!* I scream in my head hysterically. His image flashes before my eyes, and that makes me cry even harder. You don't survive in the epicenter of an explosion, not even as a vampire.

Flames crawl closer to me, and subconsciously I stretch my hand towards the fire. I almost touch the flame when a thought that more than anything Arthur would want me to live on crosses my mind.

I take my hand back in a flash. I get up from my knees to 'walk' away from the fire. I make it to the safe distance and collapse. I don't even try to get up anymore.

I notice Grace, who runs to me and embraces me at once. "We did it, we won," she whispers, excitement and relief filling her voice. But I don't feel the same. I don't feel anything. I mean, it's nice to know that we won, but... it just doesn't matter now. Nothing matters.

In a couple of seconds, Memphis joins the hug. We sit like that for some time, and then the guys help me to my feet, and we find Roy and our other friends. We haven't lost anyone from our group.

I look out of the window in my room and see the crystal blue sky, covered with lazily floating red and purple clouds. Rays dance behind those clouds, illuminating them. If I were an artist, I would definitely paint it. In a few moments, the red disk of the sun breaks through the clouds and becomes visible just above the horizon, moving down. Its light shines on the main building, making it scarlet. I stare at the beauty surrounding me with undisguised awe. It's the most beautiful sunset of my life. I sit on the windowsill until the sun disappears from the view, leaving pink waves of clouds behind.

I wish it was all I saw. But other than the sunset, I see smoke. Too much. Too thick.

At such moments, you realize that nature doesn't care about what's going on in your life. It rains when you wear new white pants. And the temperature drops too low when you go swimming. And it throws the most beautiful sunsets when you feel like your world is about to tear apart.

We won this battle, but I don't feel any joy. My last words to Arthur were *'I hate you.'* How could I have even said that in the first place? He's the love of my life. But he died thinking I hated him. I'm such an idiot. I will never forgive myself for that. What if I came at least a little earlier? Maybe I could've saved him. Or I would just die too. I guess it would've been easier.

According to the tradition, warriors are burned after their death. But what if they burned alive?

Tomorrow, we'll have some kind of goodbye ceremony. Seeing off everyone who left us. Too many. Some I meet personally, of some never even heard. Some whose names will be remembered by everyone, and some will be forgotten at once. Every death I've seen or brought left a scar on my heart, Arthur's death *made* my heart a scar.

I go take a shower to wipe that day off me, at least on the outside. I stand under the stream of water for a couple of minutes, staring blankly at the wall. Tears don't even fall anymore, I'm empty.

Then I go to bed and lie awake for a while. I take my communicator and scroll through the pictures of him, of us.

Well, unsaid words can't be taken back, that's true. I wish I could say goodbye, say I'm sorry, say I love him. I turn off the lights and lie in bed, staring at the wall. Soon I drift off from exhaustion.

CHAPTER 43

REST IN PEACE

I wake up at about 12 p.m. I don't remember when I slept so long the last time. The war exhausted me, after all.

At 3 p.m., the whole clan gathers outside near the forest. In the crowd, I find my friends. Grace hugs me, and I hug her back. Memphis wraps his arms around both of us, and then Roy joins. Randy stands awkwardly at the side until we invite him to join our group hug.

We stand like that for a couple of minutes. I probably should feel relieved that my best friends and their loved ones are alive. And somewhere inside, of course, I do. But I think war made me colder than I thought.

Damian comes to the front and calls for attention. "I want to congratulate you all on the end of this war. I know it doesn't look like a reason for celebration, and it really is not. What I want to say is that for now, it is over." For now..?

"We all should try our best to get back to our lives, to restore our homes, and try to mend our wounds. Tonight we're saying goodbye not just to warriors, we're saying goodbye to our friends, our loved ones, our families. Believe me, I know what it's like, and I know this feeling too well." He pauses. "This war has taken away my best friend. Someone who I had the honor to call my brother." He's talking about Arthur. I bite my lip to keep from crying. "May you all rest in peace. And may nothing disturb your rest." He nods and walks to the crowd.

A couple of others say their goodbyes, and then I decide to say my own. I walk to the front of the crowd. I blink back the tears that threaten to spill and set my voice to cold but powerful. "I want to send my respect to all the warriors that left us. Each and every one of them made history. Each of *you* did. Many of those who died I didn't have a chance to meet, and now I never will." I pause and take a breath. "I want to say my goodbye to someone who I had the honor to know, and more than just that, to fight side by side. Arthur was the best warrior I've ever known, the best leader, and... a good person. Those of you who didn't know him close enough might think he's not someone to look up to. I used to think that too. But I can assure you, he was not just a good leader, he was a friend. My friend too. He was ready to die for any of us, I know that. Rest in power, Arthur. Your legacy won't be forgotten." I'm almost unable to hold back the tears as I walk back to the crowd.

After more goodbyes, everyone turns to leave, but I don't go with the others. I stand there alone, looking at the smoldering fire.

"Goodbye," I whisper. I look around to make sure I'm alone. "I... I just wanted to say that I miss you. Already. And I'm sorry I wasn't there to save you. I wish I could've. But your death will never be forgotten, I promise you. It's just... I'm so sorry for all the wrong things I said and for the things I did. But most of all, I'm sorry for the things I never said. So... I forgive you, and I can only hope you've forgiven me, too. Rest in peace, Arthur. I love you."

My vision is blurred because of tears as I clutch his pendant on my neck. I throw the last glance at the fire and go back to the castle. Tomorrow, we'll cast a vote for a new leader. I'll vote for Eric, he deserves it.

CHAPTER 44

I SWEAR

I wake up more than unrested. I almost didn't sleep. But I go to the ballroom to vote for a new leader, anyway. To do this, we have to type the name and surname on a special screen, then the machine will count the votes. I wish everything was so easy in life. My fingers stop for just a second before entering, *'Eric Regan.'*

In an hour, we all stand in the same room, waiting for the results. My heart pounds, though I don't know why. Am I nervous that Eric won't be chosen? I'm not sure.

As an ally and Arthur's best friend, Damian took the responsibility of announcing the results. He comes to the stage at the front and takes the results from the machine.

Who would Arthur choose as a new leader if he could vote? I feel like he would choose Eric too, since he was his second in command, a good warrior, and a friend. Despite his absolutely unbearable character, Arthur actually did have quite a lot of friends, and everyone I know respected him.

I stare at my feet, lost in thoughts, and then I hear Damian announce, "According to the voting, you want to see Lorna Reckless as your new leader." The crowd cheers.

What? It can't be.

I stand still at my place as if glued to the floor, my eyes rounded in surprise as I stare at Damian. Then the people standing near me start to nudge me forward, and I make sure I did not mishear.

I go up the stage, and I'm greeted with a wave of applause. Damian calls for silence and says, "Tradition requires every clan leader to swear on blood to serve the clan they lead."

He friendly pats me on the shoulder. "Are you ready?" he whispers to me. I just shrug, unable to say a word.

"Shall we begin?" he says and the crowd cheers. As someone who just lost a best friend, he is holding exceptionally well.

Damian hands me the ceremonial knife.

"I don't know almost anything about the ceremony. What do I do?" I ask quietly and smile, suddenly amused by the situation. I guess I look like I'm holding well, too.

"For those of you who don't know," Damian says to everyone but looks at me sideways, "to make a vow one should let their blood drip onto the land – in our case, the floor will do – they rule and say their chosen vow." He turns to me and nods.

I cut my hand and let the drops of blood fall to the floor. I say, "I, Lorna Reckless..." The words come out insecure. I take a breath. "Swear to rule this clan fairly, and I swear to always rule with justice and truth. I swear to do my best to become the leader you all want and deserve to have."

Everyone applauds, and Damian smiles at me. "Meet your new leader!" he says to the crowd, and the applause becomes louder.

"He would want this, you know," Damian whispers to me. I feel tears well up in my eyes, and I blink them back. Not the time for crying. I'm a leader now. I need to be strong. For them... For him.

Everything has a beginning and an end. The end of one thing is the beginning of another. All we can do is hope that this new thing will be better. We will work towards a better future, a better life. We will let our tears fall, and then we will move on. We will heal our wounds and find new reasons to smile.

"Everything will be alright," I whisper to myself and smile. Everything will be fine. I know it.

ACKNOWLEDGEMENTS

    First and foremost, I want to thank YOU. Yes, you, the person who is reading this right now. Thank you for going on this adventure with me and reading this book. I hope you loved it at least half as much as I do.

    Thank you to all my beta readers and friends for being there to listen to me talk about my book and being the first people to ever read it and sharing your thoughts with me.

    Vika, Tanya, Ruslan and Denis, thank you for being with me on 24.02.2022 and not letting me sleep through all the fun. I couldn't wish for a better way to meet a war. That night and morning inspired me to write the whole chapter, after all.

    Thank you to my Mom and Dad for helping me with all those things I can't even describe. It would probably take me years to figure them out on my own! And even then I'd do something wrong.

    And last but by no means least, I want to thank myself. Because it was me above anyone and everyone else that made this book possible. I can't wait to share more with all of you!

ABOUT THE AUTHOR

Lera Shishova is just a girl whose mind keeps throwing different stories at her. When she isn't lost in someone else's book, music, or quite literally lost in a random city, she turns these stories into books so that others can read them too.

As a lover of fantasy and dark romance, she combines the elements of both in her books. She hopes that her books will inspire people, give them something to relate to, or at the very least keep them entertained.

Printed in Dunstable, United Kingdom